I0451112

Six Across is Murder

A Crossword Puzzle Cozy Mystery

Louise Foster

Owl Cafe Press LLC

Six Across is Murder; A Crossword Puzzle Cozy Mystery

Copyright © 2023 by Louise Foster

ISBN: 978-1-955458-14-6

This book is dedicated to
Cora, Chloe, and Jaxten
My three wonderful grandchildren.
You've brought so much joy into the world
and into our family.
I love you all and I'm so proud of you.

WHY DIDN'T SHE WAIT FOR THE DIVORCE?

I'm Tracy Belden and my crazy client just killed her husband.

She told me so when she called me at oh-dark-thirty.

Now his body is in the morgue, my client is the number one suspect, and I'm the main witness.

With the police ready to make an arrest, she changes her story and hires me to find the real killer.

How can I prove someone else is guilty when every other suspect has an alibi?

I need to solve the puzzle before my client is arrested for murder.

But what if *she's* the killer?

1

_— · —_

1 Down; 10 Letters
Clue: Affected by uncontrolled emotion
Answer: Hysterical

"I've killed him!" The high-pitched shriek from my cell phone cut through my sleepy haze.

My brain struggled to wake up, fighting to distinguish between reality and my dream world.

"I've killed him!"

My eyes creased open. My dark bedroom and cozy bed enveloped me. The clock showed one-thirty in the morning. I swallowed a groan and burrowed into my pillow. Please, let this be another dream.

Despite the caller's strident tone, I recognized the voice. It was my current client for my P.I. job, a wife who wanted compromising pictures of her husband. Since Nevada, where we live, has no-fault divorce, proving infidelity is pointless. However, her husband was obsessed with his public image.

Thaddeus Reilly has spent his entire life painting himself as a friendly, generous all-around good guy deeply concerned with his fellow people. I don't know if that's true, but I have proof he's not faithful to his wife. My client planned to blackmail her husband into giving her a better divorce settlement than the one in their prenup.

Whatever she was paying Crawford, my boss, it wasn't enough to balance out the grief she'd caused me in the past five days.

For a moment I was tempted to tell her she had the wrong number. That I was not Tracy Rae Belden the P.I. Then, the small corner of my brain that houses my sense of responsibility woke up and answered.

"Lorelei?" I whispered her name, hoping Kevin Tanner, my husband, had somehow slept through the ringing phone.

"You have to help me." Her quivering voice bordered on hysteria. "He's dead."

"Calm down. Who did you kill?" Her husband, Thaddeus Reilly, was really the only option, but I wanted to hear it from her.

"Thaddeus." Her rising wail ended an octave higher than it started.

I winced at the crescendo and pulled the phone away from my ear.

"He's dead. You have to come. You're the only one I can count on for support."

Shock coursed through me. Not at the violence between the couple, but hearing that I was her support system. She'd known me for five days.

This woman needed to re-examine her decision making, or find new friends, or possibly buy them with her divorce settlement.

I raked a hand through my short brown, spiky hair and wondered if I should take a look at my life choices. Then I rolled over and caught sight of Kevin as he slid from under the cover and reached for his jeans.

Nah, I'd stick with my decisions.

Kevin is twenty-nine-years-old to my thirty-six. He's charming, un-failingly polite, and easy-going. Together we're living proof that opposites attract.

I raised a brow. "Going somewhere?"

"You're not driving over there alone."

"Is that the chauffeur?" Lorelei's breathless but slightly more controlled voice sounded over the phone. "Bring him. He can help move the body."

Kevin's smile dazzled even in the dark bedroom. "Lorelei and I agree on something. I'm coming."

The comment that made him smile fueled my irritation to a flame. I'd introduced my husband to Lorelei twice. Admittedly, his six-foot-one-inch frame topped by curly black hair and sapphire eyes would distract anyone. However, he deserved more respect than to have this self-absorbed entitled twat refer to him as a chauffeur.

Kevin, now fully-dressed and tying his shoes, chuckled at my gritted teeth and obvious irritation.

I decided to put aside the issue and refocus on my client. "Did you call the police?"

"You need to come over right away." She spoke in a commanding tone, completely ignoring my question. "I don't know what to do."

"Call. The. Police." I gripped the phone in a choke hold. "If you don't, I will. Tell me you're going to phone 9-1-1!"

"Fine. I will." Her long-suffering tone was akin to a teenager on the verge of a tantrum. "Be here in ten minutes. Hurry."

The call ended as quickly as it began.

Why did I not believe she'd do as I asked?

I stuck my tongue out at the cell phone. Childish, I know. Putting the phone on my nightstand I stood and pointed at my husband. "I want it on record that you heard me tell her to call the authorities."

He held up his hand. "Duly noted and so sworn."

"This is serious."

"She's right." A disembodied voice spoke through our bedroom door. Marcus, our twelve-year-old Korean foster son, has a finer nose for crime and murder than any bloodhound alive. "Accessory to murder after the fact is a felony. T.R. could do hard time if she's convicted."

I swallowed a groan. Still in my pajamas, I strode across the floor and flung the door open to meet my son's serious gaze. "What are you doing awake at one-thirty on a Monday morning?"

His straight black hair, black eyes, and golden skin sent a wave of affection through me even as I fought to be stern.

"I'll vouch for you, too." Marcus, who'd grown up on the streets until four years ago when I took him in, pointed at me. "It's better to have two witnesses, even if we're both related to you. I just finished an on-line game with Steve when I heard your phone. It's not a school night. Remember? The teachers have an all-day seminar tomorrow."

The segue from crime to mundane reality was typical of the boy. "You have way more days off from school than *I* did as a child."

I would have said more but the sound of a key turning in the front door of our loft apartment distracted me.

Kevin wiggled his phone in the air. "I called Mrs. Colchester to stay with Marcus while we're gone."

Mrs. Colchester is the seventy-something landlady of our apartment building. Her unit is on the main floor. She's also as big a crime junkie as my son.

Of course, she has a key to the place. Our friend, Jack Rabi, also has a key. Kevin's former roommate, Jimbo and his boyfriend, Nathan have keys. Sometimes I think *everyone* has a key to our apartment.

The doorknob turned and the older woman sailed in on a cheery smile. "Hello, ducks. Another case gone wrong, eh?"

Her British accent added an international flavor to our little family. "I hope we didn't wake you, Mrs. C."

"Wasn't asleep; was I?" She scuttled across the living room in a bee-line for the sectional sofa. Her ever-present slippers made an odd contrast to her ankle length dress displaying the Union Jack. "Be sure to take your jackets. The lad on the telly says it's the coldest May in Nevada's history. He called for a chilly, damp night."

Were Kevin and I the only people who'd been asleep? Although, Mrs. C I could understand. She's a night owl. I was betting either sports or the British royal family was the reason for her wide awake expression.

She waved a hand as she fluffed a pillow and unfolded a light blanket. "There's naught to compare to the parades and pomp of the crown, eh? The mounted troops. The horse drawn coaches."

That answered my question. Not that I could say which member of the British royal family had been married or buried. Not that it mattered to me.

They were a world away from our home in Langsdale, Nevada, a resort town three hours north of Las Vegas. With a population of twenty-five thousand, the town's specially designed golf courses, five-star gourmet eateries, and eclectic art galleries make it a draw for the constant influx of tourists both local and international.

The presence of money, greed, and passion also kept me in steady demand as a P.I. Which is good, because that and our handyman business is what pays the rent. I also create crossword puzzles and sell them to on-line sites, but that money is hardly enough to keep me in my flavored coffee.

Marcus had inched his way into our bedroom with a covetous eye on our pillow topped mattress and luxurious linens Kevin had brought to the marriage last month. "Can I sleep in your bed until you get back? I could have nightmares worrying about you two."

As if a boy who made a rule of watching creature features suffered nightmares from anything.

I rolled my eyes at his transparent ploy as I retrieved my jeans and tee-shirt and slipped into the bathroom to get dressed.

"Sure." Kevin barely had time to get the word out before Marcus launched himself at the bed.

Moments later, Kevin and I stood in the doorway as Mrs. C waved goodbye from her position on the sofa. "Ta-ta, dears. I'll make breakfast in the morning and we'll have a nice coze about your latest snafu. I do hope it's another dead body."

On that ghoulish note, I waved goodbye and shut the door.

Moments later, my hubby and I were driving down the streets of Langsdale in the Great White Beast. Kevin's only boy toy is his nine-teen-sixty-seven pearly white Cadillac convertible with a red interior. He's buying it on payments from his mechanic.

I let myself relax in the luxurious interior. I refuse to admit how much I love the comfortable ride. "How much do you want to bet Lorelei hasn't called the police?"

Kevin snorted. "That's a sucker bet if I ever heard one. Grandma Feilen didn't raise no fool."

Did I mention that Kevin was born into a clan of international con artists? His charm, intelligence, and commanding personality made his family millions. The man can sell sand in the desert. His only flaw, for their purposes, was his conscience.

It tripped him up in a major con when he was eighteen. His morals cost the family a fortune. When you throw in a dead body, and a frame for murder, things got interesting. That's how he and I met. You might guess things didn't end well for the family, but he and I became besties. Ten years later, we're married.

The memories drifted through my mind as the nightlights of town rolled by outside the warm interior of the car. I couldn't count how many tourists came and went on a daily basis. Too bad Lorelei and Thaddeus Reilly were constant residents.

I shook my head. "How did I get picked for this assignment?"

"Clean living." Kevin slid me a sideways glance then laughed at his own joke.

Mrs. C spent fifty years running from a murder that it turned out, she hadn't committed. Marcus was a former street urchin who had done anything to survive until he tried to steal my wallet and Kevin spent his entire childhood scamming people. Compared to them I had, mostly, walked the straight and narrow road.

"I hate divorce cases," I groused. "I'd rather have a..."

My words trailed away as the reason for our nighttime ride struck me.

"You weren't going to say murder, were you?"

I met his teasing look and tried not to smile. "Of course not. I would never say that."

"Of course not."

Lorelei's address was on the upcoming block. The area remained suspiciously quiet. There wasn't one telltale flash of police lights and no sound of an approaching siren.

Though I'd expected nothing else, a proverbial storm cloud complete with lightning flashes, settled around me.

Kevin turned the corner onto a dark street, empty of any traffic but us. Although it was May and Christmas was several months in the past, only one thought came to mind: Silent night, deadly night.

If that woman had tried to move the body, we were all in trouble.

2

—·—

44 Across; 9 Letters
Clue: A disturbance or fuss
Answer: Kerfuffle

"Where is that woman?" I was beginning to think my life would be easier if I killed Lorelei myself. However, with her husband dead I had no one to blame. Though I'd dialed 9-1-1, my thumb hovered over the send button. I glanced over and met Kevin's knowing gaze.

After ten years as besties, we can read each other's minds most of the time. He raised a brow. "Planning to report a murder without a body?"

"Of course not." Okay, yes, I was thinking about it. Until he said it out loud, then I could see the flaw in my plan. "You can still drive off and deny all knowledge."

"Marcus and Mrs. Colchester would blab." He squeezed my shoulder. "Besides, what kind of chauffeur would I be to leave my lady without a getaway car?"

"How about if *I* drive off?"

He popped open his door. "Come on, Belden. Let's go body hunting."

For a man raised as a criminal, the man is annoyingly honest. "Fine. I'll go see what my lunatic client has done."

I stepped into the bright light shining above the garage. The unseasonably cool, damp air made me grateful for Mrs. C's advice. I pulled my coat tighter while I studied the carefully landscaped yard of the mega-mansion.

Brickwork covered half of the yard. A set of stone benches decorated with planters filled with bright colored flowers set off the display. Fire resistant bushes native to the desert lined the front of the house.

Kevin rounded the car. He scanned the quiet street again. Lots of street lights. No movement.

As he walked to my side, I raised my arm and pointed to the right. There was no fence on that side of the house. Before I could say a word, the lights went out.

I gasped in shock. The lack of moonlight plus the distance between the houses meant Kevin and I were in almost total darkness. In a heartbeat, I felt his hand on my arm. I also realized with a growing sense of irritation that the loss of light was no accident. Only someone who controlled the security system could have caused such a limited blackout.

"It's me!" The words came softly on the quiet air. "This way."

A wave of irritation swept over me. I gritted my teeth. "I am not getting paid enough for this melodrama."

I wasn't sure the words made it past my locked jaw. Even when Kevin squeezed my hand, I figured he'd simply guessed at my annoyance.

A flash of his white teeth in the darkness betrayed his smile. His aura was ablaze with amusement. He tugged my hand toward the sibilant whisper.

I resigned myself to getting on with this mad affair and walked forward. My eyes had adjusted to the darkness enough to make out the solid figure of my client. She was a good three inches shorter than my five-foot-nine-inch height. Neither of us had a super model profile but she was chunkier than me. Just saying.

"Watch out!" Her voice held a strident tone that made me pause in mid-step. "One of the cats got out. Don't step on her."

I held onto my patience with a slipping grip. I'm worried about a dead man and she's concerned for a feline who's probably chasing lizards two blocks away.

"Come on." From the rustle of gravel and the shift in her voice, she'd turned to walk away from us.

"Lorelei!" I'd have yelled at fever pitch except I didn't want the neighbors to call the police. Being shot as a felon would put a cap on what was already a horrible night. "Stop! Right now!"

I pulled a small flashlight from my pocket. A treasure from my son's collection of tools every professional P.I. should possess. It was an arsenal any detective would envy, real or fictional.

Acting on the vague outline of a figure moving in the darkness and the sound of her footsteps, I knew she was directly in front of me. Close enough to hear her quick breathing.

I flipped on the flashlight, pulled it up to her eye level, and grabbed the collar of her designer shirt. I'm petty enough to admit I felt a measure of satisfaction at her startled look when the light hit her eyes. "I'm done with these charades. Why haven't you called the police?"

Squinting against the brightness, she batted my hand away.

Her wide-eyed, panicked expression spread a ripple of alarm through my veins. She surprised me further when she swept forward, putting me on my heels.

"He's gone." The bitter aroma of whiskey on her breath couldn't be disguised, but the fear in her shaky voice was equally real. "The body's gone."

Drunk. Faking. Stunned. Her husband could have a number of motives for playing dead. The evidence of alcohol didn't bode well for a story that was already on shaky ground.

"Where was he?" Is what I said.

I glanced at Kevin. His face was partially lit by the cone of light from the flashlight. I wanted to share my concern, but his narrowed gaze was sweeping the nearby grounds.

Tension radiated off him in waves.

My fear increased exponentially. I again thought of calling the police, but what could I report? An escaped cat, and a disappearing corpse seen by a drunken woman?

With my flashlight aimed at the ground, our mismatched trio made its way to the backyard. We stepped onto the patio.

Lorelei reached out to the keypad on the gate surrounding the pool. A series of tones pierced the quiet. Lights flared to life from the corner of the house.

The sudden illumination scared the snot out of me. I froze in place, cursing Lorelei for playing with the lights again.

"Motion detectors."

I was so rattled I couldn't swear who said it. It might have been my client, but my money was on Kevin, whose stance reminded me of a panther on full alert.

Lorelei reached out and grabbed my wrist without looking. She pushed open the gate and pulled me forward.

I looked over my shoulder, scanning the lawn behind us as well as the length of the house. No movement. No one watching us that I could see. Then I focused on the area where Lorelei was pointing.

The pool was flat and dark beneath the night sky. The lights from the house managed to illuminate the near side of the pool and a half-dozen loungers but no further.

The woman who'd managed to annoy me for the past hour came to an abrupt halt. She caught her breath and pointed to an empty spot of ground nine feet ahead of us at the side of the pool.

"There." She edged away as she spoke, hiding behind Kevin and me equally. "He was there and he was dead."

I raked the area with my gaze. I even brought the small but powerful flashlight to bear.

No wet footprints. No drag marks. No blood.

Definitely no body.

"It was there." Lorelei's voice held a desperate note as she pushed me forward. "You find it. That's what you're being paid for."

Finding the missing body of the husband she'd whacked wasn't even in the ballpark of why she'd hired my boss man, Crawford of Crawford Investigations.

I was being paid to find proof that Thaddeus Reilly was having an affair. This would put Lorelei in the driver's seat of the upcoming divorce against her image-conscious husband.

Basically, it would be open season in the divorce courts. The fact that I had evidence they were *both* guilty only increased my irritation at the whole affair, pardon the pun.

The only silver lining I could find was they had no children. At this point, my sympathy lay with the missing cat and its sibling, a pair of gray extra-toed littermates who had the benefit of being non-shedding.

I focused on the logic of the current problem and swept my flashlight across the pool.

"Pool lights?" I asked without looking at her.

"There." Her voice sounded to my left.

"I'll get them." Kevin crossed between us, subtly forcing her to retreat another step.

I wasn't sure whether he thought I was in danger of being thrown in the pool or if he believed I'd toss her in the drink. I only wished she'd try something. Then I could call the police and turn myself in.

The pool lights flared to life in underwater brilliance. Showing... an empty pool. Nary a ripple in the depths. Definitely no corpse.

I flicked off my flashlight and studied the area again. My gaze followed the lawn until it disappeared into the darkness. The grass flowed to an open common area that ran behind the houses on this block. There was a grassy, meadow-like area on the next block also, complete with hedges and walking paths. Though some of the mansions had fences, several on this side and on the other side had none.

Shifting to face the woman, I met Kevin's gaze over her shoulder and raised a brow in a silent question. He shook his head, confirming his x-ray vision hadn't revealed any secrets. The fact that he'd been pulled into this stupidity, however willingly, added gasoline on my raging inferno.

I took a deep, calming breath. Though I knew Lorelei to be a consummate, poor-little-me actress with her blond hair and melting brown eyes, the woman was wringing her hands while trying to hide her well-endowed frame behind a decorative pole. Her gaze darted around. Furrows marked her forehead.

My defenses didn't crumble at her pathetic profile. Not only was my quota of sympathy exhausted, I'd seen her acting skills since day one. "Let's go inside and talk."

The woman's saving grace at this point was the high-quality coffee she stocked in her kitchen. Moments later we were seated around the kitchen booth with steaming mugs of the heavenly, life-saving liquid.

I'd taken it upon myself to free a selection of biscottis from the cupboard, cranberry and white-chocolate for me, chocolate and walnut for Kevin. The addition of the treats drew a frown from Lorelei.

Too bad. If she didn't want to share, she shouldn't have called me in the middle of the night. I fortified myself with a long drink of the delicious roast coffee and saluted Kevin who sat to my left. Then, I faced my client across the table. "Tell me exactly what happened, from the beginning."

The frown disappeared before a shaky breath. Trembling hands clasped the air between us. "I killed him. I didn't mean to. I didn't know it was Thaddeus. I didn't know what I was doing. I believed I was in danger."

My cynical side couldn't help but applaud the artful performance. Self-defense in a dark room is a good strategy. However, she hadn't actually answered my question. "When did he arrive home from his business trip? Did you argue?"

The man was constantly on the road to or from somewhere, which made the mechanics of having an affair easier for both parties. Reilly had been due home tomorrow... er, today, Monday night. His chartered plane was scheduled to land at six o'clock, which would have been this evening.

I took another sip while Lorelei put a hand over her heart.

"He must have come home early, completely unexpected." She dipped her biscotti, tossing a stiff look at me in the process. She'd obviously missed the class on sharing in kindergarten. "I was up late reading. I heard a noise downstairs around midnight. The security alarm didn't go off, so I figured it had to be Thaddeus. He has no consideration, coming home with no advance word."

Almost like he lived here. Go figure.

Lorelei twined a hand through her hair as she continued. "I went to the top of the stairs and yelled, but he didn't answer. There were noises in the kitchen, but I wanted to avoid an argument. So, I went to my room and finished my drink."

She hadn't mentioned seeing lights go on. Walking from the front door through the sitting room and past a lounge, the main hall turned more than once. With no direct route to the kitchen, why wander around in the dark in his own house?

"Did the lights go on?" I put down my coffee as she shook her head.

"Were you out of town or away from the house recently?" The question matched my thoughts but it was Kevin's voice.

Lorelei blinked at the intrusion into her monologue. She drew herself up, putting on a mask of innocence. "I needed to get away. I booked a week at a spa in Tahoe. I was gone the last few nights, but I decided to come home. I was too distracted to relax."

Time away from a mansion? Then she got tired of a spa? What a life.

It never struck her to call the police in case a burglar had been casing her empty house and thought the place would be easy pickings? Admittedly the alarm hadn't gone off. But who wanders around their own house in the dark? "What did you do then? Did lights go on?"

"Thaddeus doesn't turn them on." She rolled her eyes as she spoke. "He considers it a challenge and he's constantly ranting about the waste of energy. He's lived here for years. Blah, blah, blah."

I stand corrected.

"Anyway," she continued. "I sat in bed, sipping my drink, and fuming at his behavior. He walks in without warning at midnight. I decided to have it out with him. After all, you have the evidence of an affair."

On both of you. I kept my face neutral. "Yes."

"I went down the stairs that lead to the kitchen. There are night lights along the hall, so I didn't have to turn on the overhead light." Her hand tightened around her coffee mug. Her eyes, a hazy sandy color, grew distant. She drew a shallow breath.

Even I had to wonder if she was *this* good an actress.

"I saw his figure and heard some rustling by the kitchen counter. There was a glimmer of lights and a clicking noise. I stopped at the landing and said, "Thaddeus, we need to talk." I barely got the words out, when there was a... crash? Or... a drawer slamming shut. The flashing lights disappeared. He spun around and ran out the French doors."

I stared at the woman, speechless for one of the few times in my life. I unlocked my jaw, wondering what to say. Are you nuts? Are you making this up as you go? "What did you do then?"

She slapped her hands on the table. "I ran after him."

The woman eyed me as if I couldn't have asked a stupider question. Honestly, I had to concede the point. If someone ran, you chased them.

Kevin lowered his cup after taking a sip. He touched my forearm with the back of his hand. "Did you see his face at any point before he ran out of the kitchen?"

Lorelei scoffed at his question. "It was too dark and he was wearing that cheap mackintosh with the hood up. Once he hit the patio, the outside motion detectors popped on."

"He still had the hood of his jacket pulled up?" I didn't know how that fit in. I really wasn't sure what to ask at this point.

She thought for a moment. "Yes. I screamed at him to stop. That's when he did a one-eighty, lowered his head, and ran straight for me. He looked like a charging bull. I panicked and grabbed the bat the maid's children left behind when they were visiting last Sunday."

The picture formed in my mind like a movie on the big screen. My brain refused to let go of him keeping his jacket on. I wanted to ask about it again, but I didn't want to sound like a broken record. Why didn't Reilly toss it in the closet or hang it up when he came in?

He didn't plan to stay. That was a new angle. Lorelei hadn't mentioned his luggage. Was it by the front door?

Kevin leaned forward, eyeing the other woman as if it were only the two of them. "Go on."

His calming voice seemed to settle Lorelei's nerves. She took a deep breath. "That's when I realized this might not be Thaddeus at all. I panicked. The bat was in my hands and I swung at him as hard as I could."

She grimaced. Her hands covered her mouth as if she were gagging. "It was horrible. The dull thud. He turned and stumbled. Then, he collapsed by the pool."

I reached across the table, stopping short of touching her arm. "Did you check his pulse?"

"In his wrist." She pointed to her hand in case I wasn't clear on anatomy. "My hands were shaking so much I could barely control them, but there was no pulse. That's when I ran inside and called you."

A couple of points. Have you ever tried to find your pulse? I've tried several times. It's hit or miss and I know I'm alive. Take a panicked, shaking woman with whiskey breath and I have serious doubts about her testimony regarding the lack of a pulse.

Adding fuel to my skepticism, was the missing body. Thaddeus Reilly is a big man. He stood... stands? Five-foot-eleven. Two of me could hide behind his wide frame.

I'm not judging. I have an eighty-three-year-old grandfather and a couple of uncles with the same build. My point is that Lorelei's husband has the profile of a beached whale. I have pictures to prove it. Again, not judging, but there is no way my client moved Thaddeus's body without a lot of help.

That line of thinking led down a road called conspiracy. However, Lorelei already stated I was her support system. Why call me if she had someone else waiting in the wings?

It's easier to believe her husband had a thick skull and recovered while Lorelei was inside. Dazed from the blow, he wandered away.

I believe in following the line of least resistance. Although, that meant we had a missing man, possibly injured. "How long were you inside when you called me?"

The other woman tapped a red-and-white polka dot nail on her lip. "I poured myself a drink to steady my nerves. It might have been a double. It took me several minutes before I was calm enough to call you."

She was hysterical when I answered the phone. At no point had she called the police. I bit my lip before I responded. "Was that your first drink of the night?"

She looked me in the eye with a puzzled expression. "I had a martini with the salad, a wine with dinner, and another with dessert."

She'd also mentioned she'd been drinking when she heard Reilly at the door. That was before the last whiskey. Was that five? I was beginning to lose count. Whatever the total, she was hardly an unimpeachable witness.

"Go back to the lights you saw on the kitchen counter." An urgent tone underlined Kevin's curt question.

I'd intended to circle back to the lights and the clicking. It seemed odd when she mentioned them.

"Where did you see them?" he asked.

She pointed to her left. "By the end of the island above the drawer."

A deep hole formed in pit of my stomach. I rushed over to where she indicated.

Kevin was hot on my heels. He jerked the drawer open.

My eyes bulged out of their sockets.

A complex array of wires met my gaze. A cell phone. A small gray block of some kind of putty. And a clock counting down from ninety seconds.

3

— • —

17 Across; 9 Letters
Clue: A violent outburst of noise, light, or anger
Answer: Explosion

A bomb.

My breath left my lungs in a woosh. A burst of adrenaline threatened to burst my heart out of its steady rhythm.

"Run!" The yell came from Kevin's and my throats simultaneously.

We turned as one toward a bemused Lorelei. Grabbing one arm each, we bolted for the open French doors then raced toward the front of the house. I could only hope the cat was in a far corner of the house.

"What?" The woman had no choice but to run with us or be dragged.

Neither Kevin nor I paused to answer her question. I did manage to grab my phone. It took all my concentration to run, keep a hold of my client, and hit the speed dial for 9-1-1. However, I did it.

Yes, I have 9-1-1 on speed dial. I've learned from past experience to be prepared.

The dispatcher picked up as we rounded the front corner of the house at a dead run. Good thing Lorelei doesn't like live-in servants.

I shouted the address into the phone. "There's a bomb!"

Kevin dropped Lorelei's arm and pivoted toward the car. "Go!"

I didn't have time to think what his plan could be. "Send the bomb squad. Send firefighters. It's going to blow!"

A loud, steady car horn split the quiet street. A blazing panel of red lights lit up the fins of the Great White Beast as the engine roared to life.

I kept Lorelei running, stumbling, anything to keep her moving. My heart clenched as we passed the house next door.

Silent night. Deadly night. The phrase returned.

My gaze swept the length of the street. Yet even as my lungs seized at the thought of the people asleep in their beds, the honking horn changed from a steady assault to an even more obnoxious rhythm.

Lights flared on in the windows.

The woman with me stumbled.

I pulled her to her feet.

A man thrust his head out of an upper story window, yelling I know not what.

I didn't try to understand. "Get out of the house! There's a bomb!"

His shocked face was imprinted on my mind.

I saw him turn and run. I kept screaming at the top of my lungs.

More house lights. The erratic beat of the car horn. The white reverse lights turned red. The pearly white car shot forward. Kevin was yelling out the window.

I couldn't believe ninety seconds could last this long. My heart pounded in my chest and in my ears like a giant, numbing gong. What if I was wrong? What if we'd misread the situation?

Sirens sounded in the distance.

"Stop!" Lorelei dug in her heels. "Why are we running? What are you yelling about? Are you crazy?"

Her dead weight, combined with my thudding heartbeat, caused me to stumble. I braced myself against her to avoid a fall. With my added weight pushing on her frame, she almost went down.

Don't frown at me. I never said I was noble.

I pulled her upright. By the time we stopped, we'd regained our balance, if not our breath.

Spinning on my heel, I eyed the Reilly house. Silent and secure in the night. "We weren't wron—"

A whoosh of air seemed to steal the oxygen from around me. Then, the white blaze of an explosion and an ear shattering blast of noise. A pillar of light shot outward. Smoke and flames lit up the night.

An analytic corner of my mind froze the image as the blast blew out the back of the house. I didn't know why, but something about the image bothered me.

Sirens echoed through the streets, cutting across my thoughts. Red and blue flashing lights accompanied the arrival of two, no, three police cars. A firetruck roared in behind them.

I sucked air into my lungs as the noise added another layer to the existing chaos. Unlinking my arm from my client, I stepped forward. My searching gaze sought for the Great White Beast. If Kevin were anywhere, he'd be with that blasted car he loved.

I saw him two houses down on the other side of the street. Relief filled me. He'd turned the car around so it was facing in my direction. Standing outside the driver's door, he patted the hood of the car.

Grinning in spite of the circumstances, I let myself drown in his eyes and his smile. He was safe. We were safe.

If Thaddeus Reilly is really dead, can I be done with this case?

A pair of fierce claws seized my arm, knocking me off-balance as my client grabbed me. Her mouth was moving, yelling words I couldn't hear.

I stared at her as if we were starring in a silent movie.

If I smack the snot out of Lorelei Reilly, would I get in trouble or could I blame her injuries on the explosion?

In the next heartbeat, I realized I was too late. My moment of opportunity had passed.

Lorelei, still holding my arm in a death grip, put her lips close to my face. "Do you think Thaddeus is dead?"

A bat to his skull. Bleeding on the brain. He might have wandered away while she was inside the house only to collapse later. "It depends how hard you hit him. If he was injured badly, he couldn't have gone far under his own power. The police will find him."

Her clawed hands started crawling up my arm. "I don't want to get into trouble."

"Then you shouldn't have whaled on him with the bat." I screamed at her and yanked my arm out of her grasp. I was so done with this woman. "We need to tell the firefighters there's probably no one inside the house. Oh, no, what about the second cat? I hope he's safe. We have to tell the police to be on the lookout for your husband. He could be unconscious."

She started to back away. "I'm not talking to anyone."

Seriously? She smacked her husband. Her house exploded. Now she intended to just walk away and what? Buy a new wardrobe in New York City?

My peripheral vision caught sight of Kevin striding toward us. He held up a hand to get my attention. "I told the guys the place should be empty, except for a frightened cat."

Without slowing down, he deliberately walked between Lorelei and me. He put an arm around my shoulders and pulled me into a close embrace. A favor I was more than happy to reciprocate.

I was also happy to lose myself in his kiss. Then I leaned my head on his shoulder and relaxed.

The choreography of the firefighters and the police was a well-practiced routine. Unfortunately. My gaze followed the men and women and their hoses into the house.

My gaze narrowed. The entrance with the Georgian columns remained intact. I stiffened in Kevin's embrace. Localized damage.

Lorelei's harping voice sounded in the background like an annoying TV commercial you've learned to ignore.

I studied the profile of the blast. Stepping back, I met Kevin's knowing gaze. He'd seen the same thing I did.

Did I mention our friend Jack Rabi? A lean black man in his late fifties, he'd been my delivery man for my former job mailing packages. In his previous life, he'd been a squad leader with Special Ops for twenty-two years.

Marcus adopted Rabi as a surrogate uncle within days of moving in with me four years ago. He'd pumped the man for every combat story he knew. Attack strategies. Field maneuvers. If there was a combat technique, Marcus quizzed the man on it. More than a few involved explosions.

I'd heard all the stories. The ones that came to mind now were the ones that featured demolitions. Another memory surfaced of a gas explosion when I was young. The blast had reduced the main house to rubble and damaged the houses in every direction for a city block so badly they were unlivable.

"Localized damage." Considering the noise on the street, my voice didn't carry beyond Kevin, who nodded. Our race to wake up the neighbors had evidently been for nothing. They were never in danger. Mr. Reilly had wanted to destroy something inside his own house and nothing more.

With the picture of the fire and smoke and debris climbing into the night sky seared on my mind, I stepped out of Kevin's arms and faced Mrs. Lorelei Reilly, my client.

Or was she? If her husband was dead, the divorce was a moot point. However, I had one more thing to do. I clamped my hand around her upper arm and locked my grip.

"Ouch!" She looked at my hand as if she'd never seen it before. Shaking and twisting, she fought to dislodge my hold. "How dare you."

I pulled her up short and thrust my face forward until we were nose-to-nose. "We're going to speak with the police. *Now*."

As she recoiled, she cast a silent appeal to Kevin, complete with pouty lip.

I stabbed at her with my finger. "Don't you say one word to him. He is *not* going to save you."

Especially not from me. He's *my* knight. I turned her on her heels and walked to the nearest black-and-white police car. When a young black woman in uniform stepped into our path, I identified myself and Lorelei. In turn, Officer Ingall, as her nametag read, escorted us to the officer in charge.

Lorelei tapped me on the shoulder. "Could you loosen your grip? This is going to bruise."

I'd almost forgotten I had a hold of her. I concentrated on relaxing my fingers. After all, Kevin was walking on her other side. She couldn't run off. With my hand on her back to avoid flight, I took a deep breath. Once we spoke with the police, I'd see where I stood.

Lorelei leaned toward me. "What are we going to say?"

I frowned in confusion. What was she talking about? Then the meaning behind her words struck me. "We're going to tell the truth. The whole truth. What you saw. What you heard. When you heard it. Everything."

As the words left my mouth, the rush of adrenaline evaporated. My feet dragged. I struggled to concentrate in order to step over the hoses strung across the street. What time was it?

Midnight. That's when Lorelei said she first heard noise downstairs. No security alarm, which pointed to Thaddeus. Although, any alarm could be short-circuited.

He came home. She stewed for a while before confronting him. He ran. She chased and belted him. He fell. She panicked and went inside to drink some liquid courage. She called me at one-thirty-three.

That's nowhere near one-and-a-half hours of activity.

I slid a sideways glance at the woman. "When did you first hear the noise downstairs?"

She twined her fingers together. Her eyes were focused straight ahead, eyeing the police in the street. "Around twelve-fifteen. Twelve-twenty."

Make up your mind! I sucked in a breath of anger. What an artless liar. "When we spoke in the kitchen you said you heard someone downstairs at midnight."

She waved away my anger with a flick of her wrist. "I didn't look at the clock right away. I just glanced at it as I grabbed my glass. I was distracted. The ice had melted."

I stewed between not *wanting* to believe her because I disliked her and accepting the answer since I knew her priorities. Slowing my steps, I decided to rely on my failsafe lie-detector: Kevin.

One of the many lessons his family of international grifters taught him was how to lie, how to tell if others are lying, and to never, ever admit *he* was lying. In the face of any evidence that is produced: witnesses, pictures, recordings - deny everything.

So, I let Lorelei walk ahead and stepped to Kevin's side. I raised a brow and shot him a questioning glance.

His slightly amused gaze remained steady. "The truth. No hesitation. Her eyes never wavered."

"I'm going to... " My breath hissed out between my clamped teeth. Billows of smoke filled the sky. At this point, I couldn't prove her story or not.

I gritted my teeth and returned to my original problem. A twelve-fifteen arrival left the missing time at seventy-five minutes. Longer than I liked but depending how long she stewed before going downstairs to confront her husband and how long she drank after she hit him the time frame was more plausible.

Except I was done with this case. Whatever questions lingered regarding the attack, the bomb, the fire –

What was Reilly trying to destroy?

No! I screamed at my puzzle solving brain. Tonight's affair was not my problem. Definitely not.

I was done. Right?

4

—·—

6 Down; 5 Letters
Clue: Employed to accomplish a specific task
Answer: Hired

From the front seat of the Great White Beast, I gazed at the rising sun. The gold and pink layers of dawn put me in mind of the flames devouring the Reilly house. Perhaps the Reilly family drama was consuming me.

I stared out the window and fought to concentrate on the purple mountains painted on the horizon. Despite our long night, Kevin had taken the scenic route home, past one of my favorite views.

"I love living in Langsdale." The resort town had so many cultural aspects to draw in the high-dollar tourist. Yet it retained that small town feel. "I have you and Marcus. Mrs. C and Rabi as friends and family. Life is good. I want for nothing."

Kevin turned a horror-stricken face to me. His gaze narrowed. "Who are you and what have you done with my wife? Are you a pod person? Talk. Now."

I rolled my eyes at his reaction. "Okay, so I'm not usually into the touchy, feely mode. I grant you."

His chuckle rolled over me like warm honey in my veins.

I reached over and ran my fingers through his dark hair, sweeping it off his forehead.

He shot me a sideways glance. "Does this uncharacteristically touching moment have something to do with Mrs. Reilly, who may or may not require a divorce because her husband may or may not be dead?"

Yes, for those keeping track of the players, Thaddeus Reilly's body, breathing or not, hadn't been found by the time Kevin and I left. After hearing Lorelei's story, the police brought in more people to search the neighborhood. They were still searching when we left.

Determined to ignore Lorelei and her problems, all of her own making, I gave my hubby a tired smile. "Ten minutes with that woman made me appreciate my life choices. While I admit to my share of mistakes, I will never have to worry about having someone help me get more alimony."

Kevin snorted. "That's because we have no money or property. The only decision we'd have to make is who gets custody-"

I held up a warning hand. "I'm keeping the bed."

"So you've told me from day one." He didn't mention the unfairness of my decision since he'd brought the high-priced, pillow topped bed and the gorgeous linens into the marriage. "I was referring to Marcus and Rabi."

I had to laugh. Though our son was twelve and our friend was in his late fifties, they were inseparable. "First we have to get Marcus's adoption behind us."

"We will." Kevin spoke with absolute certainty. "Very soon."

Fortunately, after four endless years, the red tape seemed to be coming to an end. Taking a child off the street hadn't been nearly as difficult as proving who that child was at birth. Or where he was born. South Korea? North Korea? The United States?

Evidently, Kwan Ho is a rather common Korean name. Throw in a few spelling variations, Kwang How, Kwang Hough. You get the picture. Then, of course, the pertinent facts are coming from the muddled memory of a child who'd been on his own from the age of... four? Five? Take a guess.

Marcus's memories consisted of vague images. A group of people. Then, three men and maybe a woman, possibly. Screaming, yelling, repeated blows, hunger. Then he was on the streets. Alone. Had he been with family? Smugglers? No one knows. His age and birthdate aren't even certain. They came from a slip of paper he'd guarded over the years.

Now the end seemed to be in sight. Thanks to my and Marcus's white knight: Kevin Tanner. My hubby is the nicest man I've ever met. However, when he wants something, he's an unstoppable force. He's a charming, intelligent force who won't take no for an answer and, unlike me, he never loses his temper. It's impossible to be angry with him because he won't fight. It's borderline annoying except for the fact that I love him so much.

Due to our marriage, he now has a legal reason to fight for this adoption. YAY! The case worker adores him, but neither she nor her supervisors can get rid of him or his calls multiple times a week.

Last week I found a charge for a local florist for over a hundred dollars. No bouquet had landed on my doorstep, mostly because Kevin knows I can't get past the thought of paying for flowers that are going to die. Ice cream is the way to melt my heart.

When I mentioned the charge to my hubby, he told me he'd taken bouquets to the social work office on his last visit. One for the social worker, the supervisor, and the office staff. He's wonderful, but he wasn't going away until he got what he wanted.

Kevin taking over the whole adoption process had proved to be one of the many benefits of marrying him. Whenever he spoke with the powers in the bureaucracy fortress, I just sat back and smiled.

"Don't worry," I told him. "Rabi and Marcus have both told me more than once they come as a pair where custody agreements are concerned."

"And they're waiting in the apartment." Kevin slid the car next to the curb in front of our building.

Rabi's delivery van was directly in front of us.

I hoisted myself onto the sidewalk and stretched the tired kinks out of my body. A moment later as I climbed the stairs to the outside door, I had my arm around Kevin's waist and was unashamedly leaning against him. "I hope our maid has breakfast ready."

The door to our apartment was unlocked. That unsurprising fact paled next to the sweet aroma of mango coffee that swept over me as soon as I stepped inside.

I groaned in delight. "I could close my eyes and follow the scent to the coffee maker. Thank you, Mrs. C. Hey, Rabi."

The lean black man raised his steaming coffee mug in salute. He topped Kevin's six-foot-one-inch height by a bit. He had the skeletal profile of a cadaver and ashen toned skin. His shoulder length hair fell in perfect waves.

Mrs. C was bustling in the kitchen as I filled mugs for Kevin and me. I stopped to inhale the warmth and scent of the life-giving liquid.

Kevin brushed a kiss against my cheek as he picked up serving dishes full of scrambled eggs, fresh blueberry muffins, and cinnamon apple scones.

"Oh, ducks, you've timed it to the dot, you have." Mrs. C sounded as if we'd won the sweepstakes.

Which is how I felt. With the assortment of food and my empty belly, I preferred a nice hot breakfast to any amount of money.

Only when I sat at the table, did I notice the two whiteboards set up to one side. I raised a brow at my misguided child. "What are those doing there? I hate to disappoint you..."

Honestly, I wasn't broken up that the Reilly case was over, but as a caring mother I felt obligated to cushion Marcus's feelings.

"This case is officially over." I spooned a generous helping of scrambled eggs mixed with onions, peppers, and cheese onto my plate. "I'm thinking if I get the report filed this morning, I can call it closed and move on to better things. Belden and Tanner handyman services have rooms to paint and drywall to install."

Having thrown down the gauntlet, I left the matter in Marcus's court and started eating.

The boy, whose obsession to be a P.I. far outweighed every other consideration in his life, looked appropriately outraged. "You have to give a full report. You can't make that..."

We all waited while he sought for the correct word.

He pointed at me. "Unilateral decision."

"Can to," I shot back. "I did what I was hired to do. I have the pictures to prove it."

Having taken a bite after he finished speaking, he swallowed. The smug expression on his face telegraphed his determination to have his way. "You are duty bound to report on the matters of the case to the Belden Agency."

I opened my mouth to respond, but I never got the chance.

My boy child leapt to his feet. His chair screeched on the floor as he pushed it back. "Their house blew up! We heard it on the feed. If you don't start talking, I'm putting Kevin in as the official reporter."

I couldn't believe my luck. I finally caught a break. "Go ahead. Get the information out of him. That way I can finish my breakfast."

Since my hubby, Mrs. C, and Rabi had been steadily munching away, they were ahead of me in the eating department. Having lobbed the ball to my gorgeous other half, I bit into an apple scone and cast him a triumphant smile.

Marcus sat. "Kevin, she's too stubborn to deal with when she's hungry. You talk."

"Belden does love her food." Kevin's affectionate glance was almost enough to make me forget the meal. He smiled as I sent a kiss in his direction. "She's had a long day. I'll bring you up to date on what we know."

My main man gave a clean, concise rundown of our early morning adventure, complete with annoying client, missing husband, bomb, and associated chaos.

"Last I heard, no one was hurt." Kevin speared a sausage, took a bite, then pointed his fork at Rabi. "Directed explosion. Localized damage. Blew out the back while the front of the house was undamaged."

Rabi's eyes narrowed. "Professional."

His tone left no doubt in his judgment.

The single word sent a tingling spark down my veins and into the tips of my fingers. "What are the Reillys up to?"

Marcus's smirk of triumph reminded me of the Cheshire Cat. "I thought you were done with the case. You did your part."

He had the teasing, sing-song rhythm down perfectly.

I couldn't help but smile. "I can be done with the case and still be curious."

My son put his fork down. "I'm posting the facts of the case on the board. My gut tells me there's more going on with this case."

Kevin tapped his plate with his fork. "After we eat."

Mrs. C folded her hands on her belly. "Perhaps the case isn't done with us. I think you're on to something. Tack up the details when we're done."

"Do what you want. I'm going to finish my meal then load the dishwasher." I pushed aside the roiling in my gut and the questions in my brain to grab a warm muffin. As I reached for the butter the theme song of the old *Dragnet* TV show sounded from my cell phone. My hand stilled in mid-reach. "That's Crawford's ring. I have a bad feeling about this."

Marcus rubbed his hands together.

Crawford is my boss man for Crawford Investigations. He's a retired homicide detective who opened his own P.I. business. I've known him for fifteen years, worked for him for eight years, seven as a researcher. Slightly over a year as a solo investigator.

Silence descended as I swept my thumb across the screen. "Hello?"

"Why do you always make trouble?" Crawford's gravelly voice had a room clearing blast that could be heard a block away.

Holding my phone at arm's length, I jumped in quickly so I could get my claim on record that I was done with this case. "I'm ready to send the Reilly report. I have the evidence Lorelei wanted which proves Thaddeus is cheating. I'm done."

"They found the body. Lorelei-"

I gasped so hard I almost swallowed my tonsils. "Lorelei's dead? How? When? She was with the police."

"Lorelei found the body, you twit!" Crawford's outraged blast had enough force to launch a rocket to the moon.

My brain clicked in before he uttered the twit judgment. Although his words did smack me back to the real world. "I don't know what I was thinking."

"Lor', you've been awake half a day, luv." Mrs. C, her pale green eyes narrowed in thought, hung on every word. She clicked her tongue. "Not in the clear if she's found the body after laying on the wood, is she now?"

"Give the Brit the prize," Crawford bellowed. "She's thinking straight."

I didn't have the energy to try for a comeback. I gave Mrs. C a thumbs up and clicked my mind over to the logistics of the crime. "Where did she find the body? Did the police question her at the station?"

My phone was about eight inches in front my face. I spoke into it as if we were Skyping. After all, I only had the one set of eardrums and Crawford had proven himself far too volatile.

A metallic creak sounded over the line. The noise came from Crawford's ancient desk chair that he'd commandeered from the police station when he retired. He literally rolled it out the front door while his captain watched.

The rustling of paper sounded from him reading his notes. The dinosaur was old school. He preferred to put pen to paper. "Lorelei went downhill quick once the police started to question her."

"Downhill or good acting?" You be the judge. I leaned toward the latter. However, as I bit into a moist blueberry muffin, I had to admit the woman had lived through a long night. Intruder in the kitchen. Whack a man with a bat. Husband dead. Body gone. House explodes. Anyone would be reeling after that laundry list of blows.

Crawford grunted at my dig at our client and continued. "The cops drove her to her sister-in-law's house. It's three blocks from the Reilly's former home, a straight shot through the yards and the common area."

Silence had descended on the kitchen table.

Marcus looked ready to climb across and grab my phone.

Crawford spoke in the steady tone he'd used during his days on the force. No conclusion until all the evidence was in. "Your buddy got hysterical."

My buddy? No way. Hysterical? Possibly.

"The lead on the scene got the basic timetable." Crawford's decibel level was tolerable for now. "The facts jive with yours, so he drove her to the sister-in-law's house. They rang the bell together. He tried to break the news, but Lorelei went full throttle into weeping. Threw herself on the couch, the whole bit."

I scanned the jaded expressions at the table. "The woman loves to be in the starring role. I take it she recovered after he left?"

The clock on the microwave showed it was seven-fifteen. Kevin and I had left the scene not long ago.

"Bingo." A cynical note came through loud and clear in Crawford's tone. "The sister-in-law..."

More rustling of papers.

I searched my memory for the name. "Tiffany Sweet, Thaddeus's younger sister. Widowed twenty years ago."

"If my P.I. had filed a report-"

"I *did* file a preliminary report with all the basic facts." I stabbed a finger at the phone while casting a questioning glance at my son. After receiving a confirmatory nod, I pumped a fist in the air. I love getting one up on Crawford. "You need to read your e-mail and keep up on your workload."

"Don't take credit for the kid." Crawford shot down my defense without hesitation. "His reports are more coherent than yours ever were."

The glare I sent my son brought only a burst of laughter, which he tried to stifle behind his hands.

"As I was saying." A sharp snap of a paper pulled my attention to the phone. "Tiffany Sweet was shocked on hearing the news of her brother's death. According to her second interview, after the officer left, she went to the kitchen to make coffee. Lorelei was laying on the sofa. Ten minutes later, Tiffany returned to an empty room and an empty house."

I struggled to wrap my head around this scenario. Even knowing Lorelei for five *long* days, her actions didn't make sense. "After being awake all night, she decided to go for a *walk*?"

Another squeak sounded over the phone. I could picture Crawford hunched over his desk, stabbing his meaty finger on his blotter. "Her story is that if Thaddeus was hurt and confused-"

"After being smacked with a bat by his wife," Marcus interjected.

"He might have headed for his sister's house." Crawford spoke as if no one had interrupted. Honestly, it's the best way with this crowd. "Lorelei headed cross country, walking between the houses, and through the common area. Her ruined house was her target. She claims she was worried. If he was injured, he'd need help."

"I can't fault her logic." No matter how suspicious her actions appeared. "So, she goes looking for him and she happened to stumble on to the body."

"Halfway between the houses." Crawford supplied.

I brought up a mental map of the neighborhood. "The small gully behind the playground. There's a row of hedges. It's the only place he wouldn't have been seen instantly."

"Wow. Another coincidence." Kevin's flat tone made the comment more incriminating rather than less.

"Mm-hmmm." Crawford intoned. "It's not looking good for your friend."

I wish he'd stop saying that. I wanted *more* distance from this woman, not less. Breath hissed through my clenched teeth. In the next heartbeat, I put aside my personal wish to be done with the crazed Mrs. Reilly. "How did he die?"

"*Several.*" Crawford paused for impact. "Several blows to the top and side of the head."

"Ick." Not a pleasant picture. "What about the back of his head where Lorelei hit him?"

A rustle of papers sounded. "No mention of an injury in that location."

Kevin frowned as he tapped the table. "Reilly was unconscious. That's a severe blow."

"There should have been a bruise or a bump," I said running on the same wavelength. "He wasn't dead at that point."

"Nada. So far."

"I'll check with Wilson." He was the homicide detective who'd caught the call for Reilly's murder. I'd met him a few years ago on a previous case for Crawford. They'd been on the force together. Wilson and I had butted heads on an earlier case. Typical of my interaction with most cops.

Wondering if Lorelei's version of that night was a total fabrication, I pushed the image of the death blows aside. The gears in my brain whirred at top speed. Clues to a crossword puzzle. The map of the houses. The timetable for the night. "When did the police take her to Tiffany's?"

Crawford released a long, slow breath. "Six-o-five. She found the body around six-thirty."

After Kevin and I left. I ground my teeth at the woman's quick release. The police keep me for hours when I get into trouble. "Whatever. The woman does hysteria well. When was he killed?"

Crawford muttered under his breath then raised his voice. "The M.E. won't commit to a time until after the autopsy. The cool weather, rainfall, damp grass, etc. Victim was only wearing a shirt, no jacket. Initial estimate is two to six hours before his body was found."

"That would mean any time between midnight and four a.m." That didn't give Lorelei an alibi. My gaze met Kevin's. The call had woken me at one-thirty. The three of us had been seated at the kitchen table by two. Cue the bomb. Explosion about two-thirty.

"Wilson wants your statements." Crawford's gravelly voice flowed like a slow stream clawing its way over a string of rocks. "Told him you'd be in later this morning."

"Fine." Kevin nodded at my questioning look. Perhaps I could dig up more details about the manner of death or the position of the body. "Reilly had to be alive to get that far from the house."

A circle of knowing stares nailed me on my speculation.

"Not that I care." I hurriedly put that on record. "My part is done. The divorce is obviously off the board."

"Absolutely," Crawford agreed. "She paid in full, but she wants the pictures. All of them."

I shrugged. "I'll attach the photos of Mr. Reilly and his amour to my final report."

The silence stretched into several seconds. "She believes you have photos of her. Do you?"

I studied my short, ragged fingernails. "I might."

"Tracy," A loud slap carried over the phone and into my kitchen. "Why do you do things like this?"

I frowned at the phone. "How long have you known me? At what point did it bypass your alleged detecting skills that I'm nosy? I don't like people, especially clients, who don't tell me the entire story. I also like to have all the answers laid out in my crossword puzzle."

"She insists she be given all of the pictures you have."

"Then she can ask me for them directly." I answered in my sweetest, syrupy tone. "Because what I do on my time is my business. Any pictures of her and her friends belong to me. Not you and not her."

Crawford's chuckle held a dark, evil note to it. "That's what I told her right after she paid off on the case."

I had to smile. The old fart had been playing with me. "So, we're done?"

Kevin shook his head. With a smile on his lips, he pointed to the others for a silent vote.

It was a unanimous no. Lorelei hadn't contacted Crawford to discuss a divorce case that would never happen. As much as I'd wanted to be finished with the woman, the murder intrigued me. More so because I'd investigated both parties. Though I couldn't see a motive for Lorelei to kill her husband.

"Mrs. Lorelei Reilly has surrendered her passport to the police." The boss man spoke in a steady tone. "She has been instructed not to leave the state or the city."

Marcus raised both hands in a victory salute.

"She also signed another contract for us to find out who killed her husband." A note of admiration crept into Crawford's voice. "She's either very smart or very stupid."

"I'm betting she's more cunning than people give her credit for." My gaze settled on a point on the far wall as I weighed everything I knew. For all her outward fluff and vapid entitlement, Lorelei was a survivor. "Did you warn her she'd better be innocent?"

"That would be the stupid part." Crawford knew me well. "I told her none of my employees cover up a crime, especially murder. I hope she knows you a tenth as well as I do or she's putting a noose around her neck."

"If she signed the contract, I'm in. Faint-hearted blondes do nothing for me." I winked at my dark-haired hubby. "My only interest is solving the puzzle."

Crawford grunted. "Full autopsy is this afternoon."

For a man of Reilly's renown, the mayor and the chief of police would demand immediate answers. "You said death was caused by *repeated* blows. Not one smack from an inebriated spouse?"

A familiar screech sounded over the phone. Crawford's office chair always protested when he leaned his heavy frame back. "The M.E. says there was damage to the top of his skull and the right side of the head, the temple area and the occipital bones."

That didn't jibe with Lorelei's version of hitting him once from the back. I had no illusions about her honesty. She could have chased her husband down and killed him in a drunken rage, but would she have chased him for a city block?

I mulled over the image. The killer brought the man down then kept beating him. Passion. Rage. "What was he hit with?"

"Murder weapon hasn't been found yet." Crawford gave the standard police response as he had during his many years as a homicide detective. "Rough edges on the wounds."

"Not a bat," Kevin muttered, referring to Lorelei's supposed weapon.

"Did he die where he was found?" I couldn't imagine anyone moving the dead man's bulk.

"No drag marks," the bossman confirmed.

"He was with someone he knew. Family or friend." All I had to do was find out if someone besides his wife had a motive and the means to kill a man who'd portrayed himself as a perfect humanitarian.

Except, no one I'd ever met was that perfect and I had the pictures to prove Reilly hadn't been flawless.

5

—.—

36 Across; 7 Letters
Clue: A study of past events, especially human affairs
Answer: History

Marcus started in on a hip swinging dance before I hung up from Crawford. He stopped suddenly and looked up. "The Memorial Day Murder."

A ghoulish tone dripped from his words.

"Memorial Day is two weeks away." I rolled my eyes at this morbid enthusiasm, then switched gears. "However, as a reminder, Kevin's and my anniversary of our first meeting is next Wednesday. It's National Barbecue Day and we're going out to a fancy restaurant."

The boy's shoulders slumped. He tapped a capped marker to his lips. "We don't all have to go, right? Cuz that's nothing but a mushy excuse for eating. I made other plans, way more fun."

Kevin smiled at our son's latest penchant for protesting displays of affection. "Belden and I are going to the Salt Mines for a romantic dinner for two."

"Good." Marcus wilted with relief. "That means Mrs. C, Rabi, and I can order in and watch a double feature of insect movies: *Empire of the*

Ants and *Arachnophobia*. Big ants and poisonous spiders. They sound cool."

My lips curled in a grimace. They sounded disgusting. I held up a hand to forestall further planning. "Did you check with them before you made these plans? Mrs. C could have things to do. Rabi might have something else in mind as well."

"No, love, I'm fine." Mrs. C dismissed my concern. "It's rather cathartic to have insects as villains."

"See?" Marcus gave me a look of utter disbelief. He shot Rabi a narrowed look while he pointed at me.

Rabi gave an infinitesimal shake of his head. "Crazy talk."

My son threw up his hands. "I know how to plan."

"Fine." I cast a smile at my friends. I'd done my best to save them, but I knew how much they both loved the boy.

"Back to murder." Marcus pointed a marker at me. "You get your reports and we'll get the facts laid out. Who profits by his death? Who had an alibi? More important, did anyone call the guy Tad? What's with calling him Thaddeus all the time? That's stupid."

I had to laugh at the oddball tangent. I'd asked the question myself only to be shot down. "I was informed repeatedly Thaddeus was the only name he responded to."

"He was known for it." Kevin pointed at the whiteboards. "We'll use one for the victim and one for the suspects. He had children from a previous marriage."

I finished clearing the table with Rabi's help, since Mrs. C did the cooking. Then I retrieved my notes. Despite what Crawford thinks, I do keep records. My problem lies in translating my information to his forms. Not to worry, I can read my own handwriting.

We came back together at the same time. That's when Rabi announced his exit. The mundane realities of having a job drew a groan of disappointment from the boy child.

"Can you come by for lunch?" Marcus asked. "We'll have the details written up by then."

After assuring Marcus he'd return, the two bumped fists and Rabi left.

Back at the whiteboard, Marcus made a point of writing the victim's full name on the board. The second whiteboard was titled suspects. Lorelei was the first to grace the list. "Does she get the goods? Life insurance? The house?"

Kevin snorted. "Currently a pile of kindling, at least half of it."

"Strange, eh?" Mrs. C's brow furrowed at the comment. "What man destroys his own home?"

Her question struck a chord of disquiet. The whole episode was odd. I filed away her comment as I flipped to my notes about the Reillys' assets. "This was Lorelei's third marriage. She had her own income from the first two that Reilly couldn't touch. One divorce. One fatal heart attack. She was thirty-one when they married seven years ago."

Mrs. C inhaled sharply. "Mid-forties is a bad age to hunt for husband number four."

I waffled my hand. "Depending how this story ends, she may not need to re-marry."

The older woman's white curls shook. She clicked her tongue. "Ducks, you're an independent spirit. For some people it's not about money, they simply can't stand to be alone."

"You're right. Lorelei needs a foil to play off of." A performance is no good without an audience. "Getting back to the money angle, she and her current husband did not mix their finances."

Marcus slid into a chair at the table. His fists were braced against his cheeks. "You and Kevin share all your money."

My laughter was involuntary. "Kevin and I don't have enough cash to qualify as assets."

Although with only one rent to pay and our B&T handyman business gaining ground, we had a solid toehold in the lower middle class.

"Besides, we trust each other." Kevin met Marcus's gaze. He made a circling gesture around the table that included Mrs. C and by default, the absent Rabi. "We're family."

"The Reillys must not have trusted each other," Marcus mused. "But they had way more stuff, huh?"

"They were both older. He was forty-five when they married. Fourteen years older than her." I laid out the facts. "He had children from a previous marriage. He wanted to make sure his two daughters were taken care of in case anything happened to him."

"Which it did." Marcus popped up. The introspective moment vanished like a soap bubble. "He be dead and somebody be rich. He must have had buckets of money."

"Definitely." I picked up the page of assets. "He owned a successful architectural firm along with multiple pieces of real estate in Nevada and California, including office and condo buildings. He had a lucrative retirement account, investments, and a seven-figure life insurance policy."

The boy child smacked the table hard enough to make me jump. "That's fast money, right?"

Mrs. C's knitting needles clicked in steady rhythm as she absorbed every word.

"The life insurance company can issue the check as soon as death is confirmed." I checked for the exact figure. "Reilly's two daughters will receive one million each."

Kevin gave a silent whistle. "Not a bad motive."

I scanned the sheet. "The policy's been in place since the girls were teenagers. They were raised by his sister after their mother died."

Mrs. C learned forward. "You've gone over the top for a case of a cheating spouse."

"I always do a background." Which was true but there was more to it this time. "I was looking for a redeeming virtue after I found I didn't like either of the Reillys. Usually, one half of a couple is sympathetic. Not in this case."

Mrs. C aimed an eagle eye at me. "Ducks, why did you investigate your own client for infidelity? You have a rather full slate as it is. Surely, there's no need to look for projects."

I gripped my newly warmed coffee cup while maintaining eye contact with the older woman. "She irritated me. I investigated her to prove she wasn't the society lady she pretended to be. I never intended to do anything with what I learned. I don't like hypocrites."

Marcus's mouth spread in wide grin at my stiff tone. He cast a knowing look at Kevin. "T.R.'s client insulted you or me or both of us."

Kevin nodded before looking at me. "It's not personal with Lorelei. Marriage and divorce are nothing but scams to her. She was trying to pull off a score."

Spoken like someone raised in a grifting family where the money is a prize to be won. Getting away with the goods was what mattered, nothing more, certainly not people.

Except I took her off-hand insult about my guys personally. Treating life as a game and people as pawns was a view I never understood. "It doesn't matter now. Let's return to motives and profit."

Kevin steepled his hands. "The real estate will run into hundreds of millions of dollars. Who inherits?"

There, I had to admit defeat. "I didn't delve into the will. Once it's filed I can check it out. Lorelei told me her husband changed it last month. He'd been increasingly distant during the last year or more. He focused even more on business than he had before. He visited his accountant frequently, traveled more. He took on advisory contracts that he had always detested. He preferred to build things his way rather than give advice that might be ignored. They rarely spent time together or entertained like they used to."

"Aye." Mrs. C's single word held a wealth of meaning. "He's planning a major change. She was on the way out, eh?"

I sighed. "Lorelei thought he was planning a divorce. That's why she wanted dirt on his affair. He was consumed with having a spotless reputation. She intended to blackmail him using the pictures that showed him cheating."

Mrs. C stopped in mid-stitch. "So, she'd have gained more with him alive than she will by his death."

Marcus jumped into a GI Joe pose with the marker pointed at Mrs. C. "Good catch. Way to look at the bottom line."

Kevin's finger tapped in a rapid rhythm on the table. "Nevada is a community property state."

Marcus wrinkled his nose. "How long were they together?"

"Seven years." I searched for the copy of the prenup Lorelei had given me. "The prenuptial agreement limited her alimony and any monetary settlement before ten years. I don't believe she expects much from the will. She had no claim on anything he brought into the marriage or any of his assets gained during the marriage."

The older woman's knitting needles fell into a rapid dance. "She'd have taken the lot if he didn't want a scandal. You had the goods, eh?"

"Finding proof was surprisingly easy." I had done what I was hired to do: get photos of Reilly cheating on his spouse. "She was a stone's throw away from having him over a barrel. Now, the will takes precedent and I doubt she'll come out ahead."

My brain was running on overload. I catalogued a few points as clues in my mental crossword puzzle, but it was early going.

Kevin stroked his chin. "Did Reilly have a history of being unfaithful?"

"Rumors of his infidelity in his first marriage is what gave Lorelei the basis for her blackmail scheme." The woman may be annoying but she looked after her bottom line. "She knew the people involved. There was talk of the first wife filing for divorce. He'd been involved with other women off and on, but no other marriages until her."

Kevin had picked up a pencil and was flipping it over his knuckles. "Did Lorelei know about his affair?"

I shook my head. "She suspected. No proof. He was careful enough in general, but not for a P.I."

Marcus filled out his precious board with the new facts.

My brain spun like a whirling top. "Is it just a bizarre coincidence that as I'm ready to file my report, the man dies? His death robs Lorelei of a fortune."

A strangled silence met my rhetorical query.

Kevin tilted his head to one side. "You think someone killed Reilly so Lorelei couldn't divorce him? It's not like the man planned his own murder."

"I know." The nagging from my inner voice far outweighed the deafening disbelief in the room. "Back to the case. If she doesn't gain financially, she has no motive to kill him. So, who did the deed?"

"Oh, ducks, it's not all for money, is it?" Mrs. C met my gaze squarely. "The man cheated with someone, eh? You've got both parties in your pictures or your proof wouldn't count, would it?"

"Boom!" Marcus smacked the table with his fist. "Mrs. C is on fire today."

"Yes, she is." I gave her a congratulatory nod. "I hadn't thought of that angle."

My boy child aimed the infamous marker at me. "Now you have to come up with names of who was in those pictures you took. What do they have to lose?"

I stared down the barrel of a grape scented purple marker. "A firing squad would be less intimidating. I could talk my way out of getting shot. Good thing I have the name and her background."

Kevin raised a brow. "You've only been on the case five days."

I flipped through my papers. "What can I say? I'm good. I researched cases for Crawford for seven years. You'd think people who are trying to keep a secret would be more on guard against security cameras. Now that cell phones record locations, getting evidence is so much easier. It's almost as if Reilly didn't care about getting caught."

My brain had nagged at me all week on that score. I still didn't have a rationale for the dead man's actions. He was too smart not to know his wife might hire a P.I. to get the goods on him.

Marcus threw himself halfway across the table. He stared at me intently over the top of the papers. "Who's the lady? Where are the goods? I need dirt."

I gave him a flat stare as I snapped the paper in my hands. "He had a dalliance with his secretary. She's single. I have her name. She knew the score. Not the type to cause a scandal."

Kevin studied the board with an intense stare. Though his expression appeared neutral, he looked as puzzled as I'd ever seen him. "This doesn't add up. Reilly had to know Lorelei would cause a scandal during any divorce. Why give her ammunition?"

"I don't know," I assured him. "But I have the pics to prove it. It's cliché but the affair with his secretary goes back several months. She's single and had no illusions that she had a future with Reilly."

A moment of silence was interrupted by Marcus slapping the table. "What else was Reilly involved in? If you need to clear his wife, we need to find someone else who hated him."

"Reilly is the perfect man." Kevin's mellow voice held a note of mockery. "He built himself a slick façade to present to the world."

Disbelief underscored his words.

"Aye." Mrs. C's eyes lit up. Her mouth curled to a knowing grin. "And the mask will melt at the first heat from a fire. Interesting to see what lies beneath."

Our little family is a cynical lot. I smiled at the thought. "Reilly's latest project is working with the city planners on the location of the new plaza. Reilly's firm was hired to build a new art gallery and boutique."

"The fight over where to build the plaza's been raging for several years." Mrs. C clicked away without looking at the needles. She could probably knit in the dark. "The new plaza is to be the poshest part of the city. They couldn't agree where to put it until several weeks ago."

"I read about that." Kevin tapped his spoon on the table. His expression cleared. "The first building Reilly ever built was the original site. It's set to be demolished. He fought for another location from day one."

I'd reviewed the articles on the subject during my background check of Reilly. "He never struck me as a sentimental type."

Marcus scratched his chin. "How does that relate to Reilly's murder?"

"That's your mother's problem. I've done my part." Kevin stood and picked up his cup. He reached for mine then stopped. "I'll bring the pot over here and plug it in. We need thinking fuel."

"I need a nap." I admitted. Marcus tapped the space beneath suspects. "His only living relatives are his two daughters, one son-in-law, and his sister. When it comes to motive, Reilly had it by the multi-millions."

Marcus added a bullet point under Reilly's name. "His daughters will be rich now. What about them?"

"Have you got any bits on them at all, luv?" Mrs. C stretched her legs out in front of her. Her newly begun knitting project barely covered her lap. Her knitting slowed then stopped as she leaned forward. Her tone bordered on impatience.

Marcus stared at me, with the blueberry marker poised.

The page with Reilly's background was in the front of my folder. "Reilly's two adult daughters, Beverly and Amy, should inherit the bulk of his estate. They're thirty-three and thirty-one, not much younger than Lorelei. Tiffany, his sister, three years younger than him, should gain by his death. I need to see the will. I also have to do more digging into his family. None of them were my focus the first time around."

Marcus busily wrote notes under each suspect's name. "We need pictures of these people. I'll print them off the internet."

As my goals in the case shifted, new questions and clues sprang on to my mental puzzle. The pool of suspects widened. The stakes increased. Not divorce. Murder.

That's when my brain smacked into a brick wall with my client's curly blond mannequin face. "I'm going to have to talk with Lorelei again."

Mrs. C's expression scrunched up at my irritated tone. "You didn't think you'd solve the case without seeing your own client again, did you?"

I shrugged sheepishly. "I was kind of hoping."

Marcus spread his arms out. "Right now? This morning? I could go with you this time. I'm a good distraction. People like me."

I was shaking my head from word one. I was *not* exposing my child to this woman if I could help it. "I need a nap. The day started too early."

Kevin snapped his fingers. "I'll buy into that game. I wasn't due for any painting until this afternoon. I'll give myself the day off."

The boy child buried his head in his hands. "You two are boring since you got married."

"This is lovely, it is." Mrs. C started gathering up her needles and yarn. "Me shows are on. Let's go, little prince. We'll get the goods while they're taking a kip, eh?"

"I'm with you, Mrs. C." Marcus brightened instantly. "The internet will have a ton of stories on a local rich guy and his kids. I'll see who he squashed on his way to the top."

Mrs. C got to her feet and shuffled to the living room where the sectional sofa awaited her. "Don't forget his daughters. Money and ambition make the blood run thin, don't they now?"

The boy child grabbed the suspect board and followed her. "Good thinking. You should check with your sources for criminal records or problems with the law. You never know."

I took a long drink of coffee as I watched the pair with their heads together. "What just happened?"

Kevin pointed at Marcus. "The kid and the Brit stole your case."

"That works for me."

"Good." Kevin enveloped my hand with his and pulled me to my feet as he stood. "I just scored a nap with my wife."

His tone of disbelief brought a smile to my lips. "Let's seize the moment before they notice."

Hours later I rolled over and opened a sleepy eye to the clock. "Almost twelve. Now that's a good time to wake up."

Kevin sighed behind me as a rustle of covers sounded. Unlike my old bed, this pillow topped wonder was too fancy for his movement to shift the entire mattress. He put his arm around me and nuzzled my neck. "Do you think they solved the case without you?"

"I hope so." I snuggled into the pillow. "As long as neither of them demand money, I'm good. They can have all the credit they want."

He laughed against my neck. "Big surprise."

Ten minutes later, we returned to the living room.

Mrs. C and Marcus were sharing a bowl of popcorn. The older woman was watching TV. Marcus was eyeing the whiteboard with the heading of suspects.

I was grateful they hadn't set out on their own. "Kevin wants to know if you two fingered the killer."

Marcus shook a handful of printed pages at me. "No way. Supposedly everybody loved him. The media says he was a great guy. Respectable and stuff. Nobody's that perfect. I bet people secretly hated him."

"On Perry Mason, it's always the one you least suspect. That would be your client." Mrs. C stabbed an empty knitting needle in the air. "Perhaps they ganged up on him. They're all guilty."

"There you have it." I waved a hand in the air with a smile on my face. I escaped to the kitchen and filled two travel mugs with coffee for me and Kevin. "I've put forth worse theories."

Kevin snorted. "Not long ago you fingered everyone involved as the killer."

I threw up my hands. "I got the right one in the end."

Marcus picked up an orange marker and added a note to the list of suspects.

"Five suspects?" I pointed at the overburdened board. "His three relatives, the son-in-law. You added a new guy?"

"The police go after the people closest to the victim." My son's gaze held a gleam of vindictive pleasure. He added a grin as if challenging me. "His daughters were estranged until the past couple of years when they came to work for him. The younger one has been traveling to San Francisco for the past two months checking on a part in a play, while drawing salary at her dad's firm. She's also a big deal in local plays. She's starred in several in Langsdale."

Mrs. C inched so far up to the edge of the sofa I worried she'd slip off and land on the floor. "Her father called her back to Langsdale this week.

Marcus found a furious rant she posted about it on a podcast. Said she'd never be free of his interference while he lived."

My interest meter sky-rocketed to the top. "That's worth a place on the suspect list. Why didn't she quit and act full-time?"

An avid gleam sparked in Mrs. C's eyes. "Her old dad had the goods on her, I'd say."

Marcus tapped a rapid beat of dots next to the older daughter. "This one, Beverly, had a successful career in New York City. Came back three years ago out of the blue."

I leaned on the sofa. "Why did they return to Langsdale after building their lives elsewhere?"

Mrs. C had a thoughtful look on her face. "If the younger one blames her father, he pressured them. Pulled them home and made them stay, didn't he?"

"Evidently, Reilly has a few chinks in his armor of perfection." Clearly, this case was going to require more digging. "What about his background? The first Mrs. Reilly died in a one-car accident."

"Got it." Marcus pulled a piece of paper from the table. "Twenty years ago, Reilly and his wife were driving home from dinner with his brother-in-law Sam Sweet. Mrs. Carol Reilly was in the front seat. Sam was behind her in the car. Reilly lost control. The car slid down an embankment and wrapped around a tree. Reilly was hurt bad, spent ten days in the hospital. The other two were killed on impact."

I took a long, sustaining drink of my mango flavored coffee. "Lorelei said his first wife was about to file for divorce for cheating on her. Any mention of that?"

"Nope." Marcus popped another kernel in his mouth. "We had to read like fifteen articles before we found out Sam Sweet died in the crash. Most of the news centered on Reilly being tragically widowed, his survival, and his injuries. The stories told about him and his nomination for some national board."

Mrs. C thrust her ruby tipped hand out, shaking it wildly. "He was in contention for a very prestigious position before the accident. Afterward, Mr. Reilly won hands down."

Kevin tapped a rhythm on his cup. "Any life insurance?"

The boy exchanged a glance with the older woman.

Mrs. C shook her head. "A bit on Mr. Sweet. Reilly collected two hundred thousand on his wife."

"Lot a money." Marcus's eyes narrowed. "But back then Reilly owned real estate worth twenty times that amount."

I eyed the dates on the board and turned to the present day. "Who's that last suspect you added? Brandon Haigh?"

Marcus pointed to the name. "The owner of an art gallery that's on the ground floor of Reilly's office building downtown. He and Reilly almost came to blows at the council meeting two months ago about the new plaza's location."

Mrs. C's knitting dropped to her lap while she studied Marcus's list. "Mr. Haigh demanded the Drake building, the original site, be slated for demolition immediately so the project could move forward."

Marcus nodded like a bobble-headed doll. "Reilly launched his career and his fortune investing in the Drake when it was built. It's a perfect location for the plaza but Reilly's fought against it being destroyed for almost five years."

I didn't see a tie to Reilly's murder. "What happened?"

Mrs. C eyed me over her knitting. "The council voted to accept the alternate location. The Drake was saved."

Marcus followed her every word, waiting to jump back in. "Haigh lost it! He attacked Reilly, screamed about bribes, and had to be thrown out by security guards. He swore he'd never quit. He threatened Reilly."

"That's bizarre. Why does he want to see the Drake destroyed?" My brain worked to catalogue the different angles of this case and how it led to Thaddeus Reilly's death. "I'm still not seeing a motive for him to kill Reilly."

"Bad blood, ducks." Mrs. C lowered her tone. The woman had seen too many noir movies. She jerked her head at Marcus. "Tell her the rest, eh?"

Marcus had been gritting his teeth to keep the story contained. "Mrs. Colchester's source at the arson squad told her there were multiple fires at the Drake three weeks ago. Turns out, they found old damage to the foundation. The council reversed its vote. Reilly was furious. He told the arson investigator Haigh was to blame for the fires."

"Several blows." That was the cause of death according to Crawford. "You're right. With their history, if Reilly went down in a fight, the other man might have kept beating on him."

Kevin scanned the list of names. "Five people with possible reasons to kill the man. Were they in town yesterday... er today?"

Marcus fought to maintain a serious expression, but his grin broke through almost instantly.

"Why are you smiling?" My shoulders slumped. "Are you going to tell me all the suspects were in Langsdale?"

Mrs. C had the grace to look sympathetic. "First glance says they were present and accounted for."

"That's great," I muttered.

Marcus tapped his chin with a smug look on his face. He was obviously enjoying the multiplying complications. "Don't worry. We'll get 'em."

A rapid tapping drew everyone's attention to Mrs. C. Her knitting needle did double-time on the coffee table. "The victim was alive at midnight. They can't all have alibis, can they?"

"I hope not." I crossed my arms over my chest. "You've both done a lot of work. I'm indebted to you."

Marcus ran over and jumped on the sofa. "Enough for a night at a restaurant? La Casa's?"

I shook my head before he finished. "Don't push it. You got this information off the internet. I could have done as much. However, I will pop for ice cream at the Silver Streak Creamery after dinner."

Marcus put away the pleading eyes. "I'll take it."

He shot a victorious smile at Kevin.

A series of knocks sounded on the door. Rabi walked in holding bags marked with our favorite sandwich place. It took a few moments to settle the food on the kitchen table and the boards in the kitchen.

Marcus's gaze was glued to his phone. "News flash on the blast. A neighbor was injured when he was thrown to the sidewalk in the blast. He's in a coma at a local hospital. There's a picture of him at the scene. His face is covered in bandages."

"I hope he'll be okay." I exchanged a glance with Kevin. "I thought we warned everyone in time."

Kevin looked puzzled. "I didn't see anyone on the sidewalk. Where could he have been?"

His question went unanswered as Marcus launched into a rapid-fire report. As we settled down to lunch, Rabi was regaled with what we'd learned.

With so many suspects, hearing the details again helped me sort out the players. Yet, my brain kept pushing me toward Lorelei. "The tragic widow."

Kevin made a show of looking around. "In this case?"

Mrs. C's British accent floated to the top as she told Rabi about the Drake conflict.

Hearing it for the tenth time was evidently my magic number. I put what remained of my sandwich on the table. "If I found out Lorelei had an affair, her husband had to know."

Kevin eyed me. "Lorelei wouldn't care about having her name in the news."

Marcus interrupted his flow of information to look at me. "Are you going to talk to her again?"

I'd made no secret of my feelings for the woman. "That's why I get the big bucks, for doing the dirty work. Besides, I've never met Reilly's sister, Tiffany Sweet. It'll be interesting to see her reaction to her brother's death."

Tiffany lived three blocks away from her brother and sister-in-law as the crow flies. The body was found halfway between. How did the two women profit by Reilly's death?

I studied the board with a narrowed gaze. "Mrs. C, what are the odds you can get a copy of Thaddeus Reilly's will?"

The older woman rubbed her hands together. "I'll do me best, luv."

"Marcus." I pointed at the boychild. "Find a map of the neighborhood, showing the houses and where the body was found."

The boy exchanged a grin with Rabi. "I'm on it."

"I'm going to see how well the widow and the sister get along."

Time to see whether my client believed she'd gotten away with murder.

6

— • —

29 Down; 8 Letters
Clue: A common understanding or feeling between people
Answer: Sympathy

Tiffany Sweet opened her front door and greeted me with puffy eyes and a strained expression. Dark brown curls surrounded her thin face, strained with weariness. "Ms. Belden, come in."

She turned without waiting and left me standing on the front step. A few steps took her past an umbrella stand with two garish umbrellas in it. She reached out a hand to the wall to steady herself as she walked into the living room.

No bother. I can find my own way. I walked in and shut the door. "I'm sorry for your loss, Ms. Sweet."

"You never met my brother in person, did you?" The other woman put a hand on the end-table. She plopped on the sofa as if her legs could no longer support her. She grabbed another tissue. "You only saw him through the lens of a camera, hiding behind a bush."

Actually, I usually take pictures from my car. Hiding behind a bush is something that will get you a visit from the police. I clenched my jaw to keep from smiling, or worse, from laughing. Some part of my personality has this perverse reaction to people who put on a holier-than-thou attitude and try to insult me.

Keeping a roof over my head and food on the table is my priority. If the morality of being a P.I. bothered me – and it didn't--the thought of Marcus going hungry or being homeless was an instant cure. I've skated very close to poverty a time or two, it's not a pleasant view. Second guessing my choices doesn't keep me up at night.

Besides, if people didn't cheat on their spouses, they wouldn't need to worry whether I was in my car watching them with a camera or tracking their credit cards. It's so convenient that people never turn the morality mirror on themselves or their loved ones.

I brushed off her dig as I stood in the archway leading to the living room. Compared to her brother's mansion, Tiffany's house was comfortable but nothing ostentatious.

"By the way, call me Tiffany. Ms. Sweet sounds like a first-grade teacher or a porn star." Her friendly tone was a complete opposite to her attitude at the door. She dabbed the new tissue at her eyes. Admittedly, this was a bad time for her. "If you're here for the she-witch, she's in the kitchen making tea."

Surprise coursed through me. Did her words contain real animosity or were they a cover? I took a seat in a stiff-backed chair.

The other woman planted her feet on the ground and raked her hands through her hair. "I know how I sound. My workaholic brother was far from a perfect husband."

I shrugged. I was from Kentucky. Family loyalty is bred in the bones. "He was your brother."

Besides, there were plenty of reasons for not liking Lorelei.

The click of heels announced the woman's approach.

My client swept into the room carrying a fully loaded tray. "From lady of the house to maid. Are we still on the sea-witch or have we moved up to the B-word?"

She tossed off the comment with a rueful smile.

Part of me admired her attitude. Like me, if the morality of her choices bothered her, she wouldn't be where she was. She certainly wouldn't have three marriages and two dead husbands behind her at thirty-eight-years-old.

Bad luck? Or good planning?

I took a measure of the two women. Supposedly grieving sister. Smiling widow. Quite the contrast. Was it too obvious?

"Lorelei tells me she knew you before she met your brother." I shot the words into the tension filled air. "Were you good friends? Or simply acquaintances?"

Tiffany raised her head out of her hands, sweeping her hair out of her eyes. She gave me a flat stare.

My client froze in the act of setting the tray on the table. Her hands clenched the handles before she completed the act. The cups rattled as the tray connected with the table. She turned to her sister-in-law. "I told you. Takes no prisoners. Pulls no punches. And, I have to say, I pulled the trigger on her."

"Then why hire me to find the killer?" I asked.

Lorelei's brows formed a vee. "If I didn't, everyone would think I'm guilty."

Tiffany threw back her head. Her eyes blazed. "They already think you're guilty."

"She doesn't." The blonde stabbed a finger in my direction. "Tracy investigated me and Thaddeus. She knows I had more to gain by a divorce than I did murder. The cops might take the easy answer and railroad me. She is too consumed with getting the correct answer to hide anything."

Lorelei knew how to read people. That's how she got her three husbands. She also wasn't done. "Tracy doesn't like me, but she won't settle for anything but the truth. I'm innocent and she's going to prove it."

Her smile held a vindictive triumph. Her logic and motives were a perfect fit for her personality. The woman was good at covering for herself. "No one is going to frame me for his death."

Lorelei crossed in front of me and sat in the other chair. With Tiffany sitting on the sofa, we formed three corners of a triangle.

Our hostess tossed her head, composed her features, and reached for the teapot. She focused her attention on the act of pouring and serving the hot liquid in the delicate china cups. Her arms shook slightly. The strain of control showed in her tight jaw. A small plate with a variety of cookies joined the steaming cup she put in front of me.

I dislike tea. However, I enjoyed the act of pouring milk from a tiny, silver pitcher and adding sugar cubes to the hot liquid to watch them dissolve. It was like being at a proper English tea party.

Tapping my teaspoon on the cup brought forth a satisfying ring. It made me feel like a judge banging a gavel. So did the reaction of the two women. "Nine years ago, you two met. How? Why? Planned, Lorelei? The only sister to another wealthy man on your radar?"

My client threw her blond hair over her shoulder. "You know my version. I'm not playing this round."

I raised a brow at Tiffany.

Tiffany finished sipping her tea with a satisfaction I reserved for coffee. Her expression looked relaxed. The tea ceremony had evidently helped her regain control.

She took a deep breath. "I met her at the same society functions. We served on various boards. We hit it off, to a degree. Lorelei is tough. A year later, I attended a charity dinner with my brother. He and I lost our spouses in the same accident years ago. He avoided dozens of snares. Lorelei was there. She was subtle. I'll give her that. He never saw her coming. Neither did I."

The woman's judgment struck me as too damning.

I noted the aroma of my tea while munching on a butter cookie. "Your brother never went to society functions. Why was he at one where Lorelei was certain to attend? You didn't point your brother in her direction for your own amusement, perhaps?"

Tiffany's eyes widened as if she'd been struck. The reaction was gone in a heartbeat, but it was telling.

The clatter of a spoon reverberated as Lorelei tossed hers to the ground. "You set me up? For what? Failure? All these years you've dug the knife in every chance you got. That I was a gold digger who set my sights on Thaddeus. You never let me forget it, Miss High-and-Mighty."

Her sister-in-law sat with her carefully crossed ankles and her polite mask in place.

Lorelei's rising voice echoed off the walls. "Thaddeus wasn't on my radar. You kept bringing us together. I wanted Phillip."

"You were never going to get Phillip." A scathing tone rang in Tiffany's voice as she raised her chin. The better to look down her nose. A sneer curled her lip. "I saw to that. I never dreamed you'd get Thaddeus. I underestimated you."

Lorelei drew in a long breath. Her hate-filled gaze never left the other woman's face. With a quick move, she grabbed the tray of cookies and threw them in Tiffany's face. "You cow."

I sat back to avoid the flying missiles.

The heavy silver tray fell to the floor with a weighty clang.

Talk about kindergarten re-visited. Or perhaps mean girls in high school.

This is what happens when you put the fox in the hen house.

I tried to push further in the sofa as I stirred my steaming tea. No telling what missiles would fly next.

Tiffany's cool mask gave way to horror.

I wasn't sure if she was appalled by the assault or by the thought of someone defaming the tea party.

Lorelei was on her feet now, fists clenched. "Your brother cheated on me within a year of our marriage and I did nothing. I honestly loved him in the beginning. It was the two of you who drove me into the arms of other men."

I winced as her screams echoed off the walls. That woman had a piercing tone when she reached the upper octaves.

Tiffany got to her feet with a slow, deliberate air. Her fingertips pressed against the arm of the sofa seemed to steady her. Then, she clenched her fists. Her dark gaze filled the air with restrained violence.

The two women faced off like boxers readying for a bout.

Would I be witness to another crime? This tired, worn-out woman would be no match for Lorelei.

If Tiffany went for the teapot, I was going behind the chair. That stuff scalds.

Tiffany pointed to her front door. "Get out of my house and out of my life."

"I have a car coming." Lorelei flung the words in her face. "I'm not traipsing up those stairs constantly because you decided to move to the first floor. I wanted to be here long enough to see Tracy go after you. I underestimated your lies and duplicity."

That was saying something coming from Lorelei. I took a nibble of my cookie and watched the drama. Now I knew how Marcus and the others felt when I confronted a suspect.

My client flung an arm in my direction. "Why don't you tell Tracy about the new will Thaddeus wrote last month? Interesting how much more you profit under this version than the former one, isn't it? How convenient he died when you were within weeks of losing your house."

Tiffany's mouth worked for a moment with no sound. Finally, she exhaled through clenched teeth. "I have resources. Besides, Thaddeus would have helped me. He always stood by me."

"He hadn't done anything to save you so far." Lorelei spoke with an evil grin. "Why would he have stepped in now? He told me more than once how you and your husband played him for a fool on your losing ventures."

As the attackers regrouped, the thick silence was broken by the chime of the doorbell. To me, the noise sounded like the gong between rounds in a boxing match.

"That will be my limo." Lorelei drew herself up. Turning toward the door, she looked at me. "I'll be at the Rupert on the Mark for the next round."

Of course, the most expensive five-star hotel in town.

I saluted her with another butter cookie as she swept past. Her heels ground a few of the fallen missiles into crumbs. Moments later, the click of the door announced her departure.

Tiffany and I stared at each other across the crumpled cookie remains littering the sofa and floor.

She heaved a sigh. "You're not leaving?"

I tapped my lips. "I have a few more questions. To be fair, I've only asked two."

Though they had proved to be doozies. I honestly hadn't expected an attack with cookies as weapons.

A raised brow met my comment.

She threw up a hand. "Fine. What are your questions?"

"Why did your brother go to such lengths over the past few years to bring his daughters to work for his company?"

Her eyes widened. "I don't know."

Evidently, she'd expected me to stay on Lorelei's background and motive.

Her gaze grew distant, seemingly heavy with regret for her and her brother's choices. She faced me directly. "My brother contacted the girls out of the blue. I was in touch with both of them. I visited them periodically. As much as I love my nieces living close by, I don't know why he did it. He never explained himself to anyone."

"Did you ask them why they returned? Was it by choice? Did he force their hand?"

The other woman met my gaze. "They never said why. I know they were happy where they were; living on the coasts, leading their own lives."

She refused to admit Reilly had somehow blackmailed his daughters to return. "He never spoke to you about contacting them? Or what his plans were?"

Tiffany slumped against the cushions of the sofa. Weariness weighed her features and her voice. "Thaddeus and I have had an up and down relationship over the years. He didn't have a lot of free time."

"When did you last speak with him?"

"Four, maybe six weeks ago." She sipped her tea, composed once more. "I found some old family papers and asked him to stop by to discuss them."

That was a different side to the hard-nosed businessman. "What were the papers about?"

A frown furrowed her brow above her sharp gaze. "Nothing to do with his murder. It was a genealogy question he'd asked me about."

"Was he always interested in your ancestors?" I couldn't fit that angle into the profile I'd built for Reilly.

Tiffany's expression stiffened. "His interest had grown over the past few years. He was getting older. He'd spent most of his life driven to succeed."

"And to look good doing it?" His reputation as a man of the people was important to him, but it seemed to be nothing but a façade. "Was he the paragon the press wrote about? Or was his reputation just for looks?"

Tiffany gave me a rueful smile. "Thaddeus liked people to think well of him."

"So, I've heard." I leaned forward. "Was your brother ill?"

"No." She shook her head. She dismissed the idea with a puzzled frown but without hesitation. "That's what I thought at first, but he wasn't sick. No terminal illness to explain gathering the family together."

"Corruption in the company? Embezzlement? The business was going under?" I pointed my half-eaten macadamia nut cookie at her before taking a small bite. "The explosion destroyed half of the house. Maybe he destroyed evidence of wrong doing."

"He could have shredded any incriminating papers." Tiffany scoffed, then she shook her head slowly. "He fought his way to the top of his profession. He would never risk losing one dollar of his money or one ounce of the respect he earned. His reputation meant everything to him. He wanted people to think well of him. He made them respect him."

Her words took my breath away. I'd trailed Thaddeus Reilly for a week, but I'd never seen what drove the man. His pride.

His work was his life.

Possibly because I had no drive to impress people or climb a corporate ladder. But I did have my pride. His reputation was as important to him as completing a puzzle was to me. "If your brother wasn't destroying evidence of corruption, why would he blow up his house?"

"I can't believe he did it." Again, Tiffany answered without pausing to consider. Her puzzled expression and sudden silence added weight that her words had been a gut reaction. "I'd like to blame Lorelei for planting the bomb, except she was in the house before it blew up. At least, according to you and your *friend*."

"My husband." An icy tone coated my words. The fact that Tiffany eyed me with a suspicious look had little effect on my reaction. My irritation stemmed from Kevin being slighted twice in one day even though I could hear his laughter in my mind. "If you think I'm in league with Lorelei, you need to step back and rethink your accusation."

Tiffany raised her chin at my uncordial reaction. The light of battle lit up her eyes.

"I don't throw cookies, and Lorelei is correct about one thing. I don't quit." If Tiffany believed I was going to back down, she'd learned nothing in our short acquaintance. I was going to get the answers. "Why are you so convinced he wouldn't have planted the bomb?"

The other woman set her jaw. She stabbed the air with her finger. "That was the first house he built. He updated it constantly. It states in the prenuptial agreement and in his will that Lorelei has no rights to it in case of a divorce or his death. He would never destroy it. It was his show piece."

Her fierce defense added weight to my own concern over Reilly planting the bomb. However, the house wasn't the only unanswered clue in my puzzle. "What was the money issue Lorelei mentioned?"

Tiffany responded with a weary sigh. "A balloon payment is due on my house. She thinks I can't pay it."

"Can you?"

"Lorelei was never my confidant." Tiffany frowned at the mess on the floor. Her expression tightened. "My husband was an inventor. Ninety-eight percent of the patents he filed came to nothing, but there were a handful that hit the mark. I live quite comfortably on the proceeds. I asked Thaddeus for the cash. Why not? When he refused, I made the payment."

I made a note to check the veracity of her statement. To paraphrase Miss Marple, I never believe what people tell me. "You and your nieces will profit by your brother's death. You'll never have to worry about money again, will you?"

"You're absolutely correct." She met my gaze squarely. "But why would any of us kill him? And why now?"

Those were the questions I'd been hired to ask.

All I had to do was find the answers.

— • —

7

19 Down; 8 Letters
Clue: A surreptitious manner; A characteristic of felines
Answer: Stealthy

"I love revisiting the scene of the crime." Marcus stopped by the side of the Reilly house and spun on his heel to face Kevin and me. He was in the same place where Lorelei had stood very early this morning.

The crime scene tape stretched behind him framed him perfectly. A somber expression covered his face as he reached into his pocket.

Kevin and I exchanged glances. We both knew what was coming.

The boy child pulled a leather flip wallet out of his pocket embossed with MBT, Marcus Belden-Tanner. Flipping it open, Marcus stuck it in his shirt pocket to display an official junior P.I. license from Crawford Investigations.

I was about to comment when Kevin's phone rang a stilted marching song. Marcus had programmed in the tune for the social worker assigned to his case. He'd been my foster son for four years now. Even for bureaucratic red tape how long could an adoption take?

"Hello?" Kevin's steady tone was not only polite, but friendly.

His unflagging sincerity was a feat I could never consistently pull off. My impatience led to annoyance which always bled through in the end. Perhaps that was why none of the many social workers who'd been on Marcus's case over the years buddied up to me.

Kevin stopped in his tracks. The plastic bag in his hand swung against his leg. His eyes widened. "Say that again?"

I exhaled slowly at the prospect of yet another delay in the adoption caused by some outdated rule that no one had ever heard about. Raising my chin, I tried to paint a brave face for my son.

Marcus's expression was resigned.

My hubby's jaw dropped. His shocked gaze met mine. "Tracy and Marcus are here. I'm putting you on speaker."

Kevin motioned Marcus toward us. "Repeat that, Mrs. Everett."

"I said, the last hurdle has been cleared." The woman was just over sixty. Her voice held an authoritarian timbre. "The adoption of Marcus Belden-Tanner, officially Kwan Ho, by Kevin Tanner and Tracy Belden has been approved. I can look at the first open dates. There are some in a few days."

I stared at the phone. My jaw dropped. The words I'd fought so long to hear couldn't penetrate my shock. Honestly, my knees almost buckled.

A piercing yell broke the spell. Marcus's high-pitched scream was enough to scare bats out of their caves. He launched himself at me, throwing me off-balance. All three of us embraced, jumping and spinning in a wild circle. I screamed at the blue expanse overhead.

Several minutes passed before sanity once more reigned.

I hadn't seen Kevin sign off on the call. He had an arm around me and Marcus.

Holding us close, he brought his phone up to his ear. "Give me the available dates and we'll let you know our choice."

I was jumping up and down with my hands over my mouth.

Marcus threw his arms around my waist and we twirled together.

"I've got the dates." Kevin's farewell sounded behind me. "Thank you."

Kevin swept us up in a hug followed by more yelling.

Several minutes later, I caught my breath. "I can't believe we got the call! After all these years, the adoption will be completed."

Marcus's eyes were twice as wide as usual. "We have to tell Rabi and Mrs. C. Wait till they hear it's official!"

With my feet finally planted on the ground, I couldn't stop smiling. Then, the wind shifted, and I caught the scent of burned wood. The remnants of the Reilly mansion bore a mute witness to our celebration. The reason for our visit returned.

Kevin followed my gaze. He patted Marcus on the shoulder. "We'll tell Rabi and Mrs. Colchester tonight. Let's get down to business."

Marcus tapped the license clipped to his pocket. Then, with a wide grin, he turned and bolted under the crime scene tape stretched between the house and the fence.

"Whew!" My son's high-pitched voice carried in the still air of the afternoon. "This place stinks! The rear of the house is gone. All of it."

I opened my mouth to remark on the value of silence while sneaking into a crime scene. Then, I realized that ship had sailed. Our scream fest would have woken up anyone within a city block.

"Marcus." Kevin's calm tone beat me to the punch even as his fingers on my arm stopped my rush forward. "Tone it down. You'll scare off the cats."

The boy popped into view above the yellow and black tape. "Did you bring the stuff? Do you think the cats are okay?"

Kevin, having retrieved the sacks dropped during the celebration, held up a plastic bag in response to the first question.

I shrugged at the second one. "They should be unhurt. Rookie was out of the house when it blew and Mr. Pickles was in the attic if he had a lick of sense."

Relief lightened Marcus's expression. "Good."

I kept my smile in place until he disappeared. "I made that up. Those cats could be in the next county by now. He'll be bummed if he doesn't find them safe."

"You're such a worried mom." Kevin spoke around a chuckle. "House cats will stay close to home even with this stench."

I rounded the building. Pieces of siding lay scattered around the pool next to blackened shards of unidentifiable debris. I grimaced as the acrid smell of burned plastics hit me with renewed force. As my analytical half geared up, another corner of my brain was hung up on the missing cats. Would they stay in the midst of this smell?

Moving close to Kevin until our arms touched, I met his gaze. "Is it too much to hope that we're giving the cats to the animal shelter?"

My hubby held up the plastic bag. "I have a quart of vitamin D milk and two five-dollar cans of cat food. This is not an investment for shelter cats."

Having pulled my camera out of my bag, I heaved a resigned sigh and started clicking away. I knew Lorelei had no interest in the cats. She'd said as much the few times I saw them in the house during our meetings. The cook and the maid fed them and emptied the litter boxes. "Maybe someone else took them to the shelter or gave them a new home. By the way, Marcus, they have their claws. Be careful if they come to eat."

"Belden."

I glanced over my shoulder in response to Kevin's tone.

He pulled one hand out of his jacket pocket and zipped it up. His other hand pointed to Marcus.

Mr. Pickles, the twenty-six-pound male cat was crouched over an open tin of seafood mix. Rookie, a mere twenty-pound female, lay in Marcus's lap. The boy had flipped her on her back and was rubbing her belly and scratching her neck.

When Rookie stretched her big, seven-toed-front-paws toward Marcus's eyes, I caught my breath. Instead of scratching him, she batted at his face prompting a giggle.

As Mr. Pickles finished his feast, he moved to Rookie's untouched food. She flipped out of Marcus's lap and blocked her littermate, hissing in his face. She attacked her food with ravenous abandon. Her brother retreated to his bowl of milk with resignation.

"Why do I even bother?" I clicked off a few shots of my son's smiling face. Then I changed angles and shot the debris field in and around the pool.

Kevin patted me on the back. "Looks like we have two more strays to add to the home count."

"Oy." I continued my circle of photos of the yard. "I want it on record that I am not doing litter box duty. We also need a scratching post. If one claw touches my sofa, those felines better watch out."

"What kind of cats are they?" Marcus now held Mr. Pickles under his front legs with his back paws on the boy's shoes. The cat's head was on my son's chest.

"Gray." In the face of my husband and son's expectant gazes, I searched for more information. "Uh. Poly- something, lots of toes. She has seven on her front paws and the boy cat has six toes on all four feet. Non-shedding, which is probably not true. Reilly got them as gifts from a business associate three years ago."

Marcus stilled, worry etched on his face. "What if the client wants them back?"

The boy vastly over-estimated Lorelei's concern for anyone but Lorelei. "She's already forgotten they exist."

His dark eyes narrowed, trying to cover all the bases. "And the daughters? They don't own them, right?"

In the face of his obvious concern, my flippant answer stalled on my lips. "Lorelei would be the owner. The Reilly daughters may not even know about the cats."

"What if they run away?" Panic underscored Marcus's tone. He tightened his hold on the purring tomcat as his gaze slid to a napping Rookie at his feet.

Was he serious? I couldn't be lucky enough to lose these felines now if I tried. "Cats have a survivor instinct. They know a good thing when they see it."

Marcus squatted and started petting Rookie. "Are there carriers for them?"

I positioned myself facing what used to be the back of the house and pointed the camera at the structure. "In the garage."

Kevin was already walking that way. "I'll get them."

I didn't bother pointing out the roadblocks in his plan. Crime scene. Taking personal property. Locked doors. They weren't sticking points in Kevin's world. He could pick most any lock in existence. As for the cats, no one cared about the furry creatures more than our twelve-year-old son. Unfortunately.

Aiming the camera at the kitchen, I took several panoramic views. Then I enlarged the focus to capture more detail.

"Got 'em." Kevin returned with two large cat carriers. He crossed behind me.

The raw destruction looked far worse in the sunlight. Yet something struck me as odd. I stepped closer to the blackened frame. The camera easily enlarged a scene through a gaping hole in the wall. The mirror over the intact living room fireplace showed a clear, unbroken surface. How could that be?

The reflection of a woman holding a camera showed up perfectly. I took a picture of myself as the metal clanging behind proved the cats were being safely secured. There went my last hope. There was no losing those felines now.

In the camera frame a pan to the right showed the candlesticks on the mantel intact and standing upright. Strange.

A few more pics than I shifted to the burned kitchen. The damaged walls. A gaping hole in the ceiling gave a clear view to what used to be the upstairs office. Shadows surrounded me, darkness dimmed the photos.

A pair of strong hands grasped my shoulders. I felt myself pulled out of the depths of the kitchen.

"Back it up, Belden." Kevin's stern voice sounded in my ear. He propelled me several steps to the rear. "This is a bomb site. It's not stable."

"I didn't realize I wandered in so far." I lowered the camera to stare at the slanted roof. The peak, three stories above the worst of the destruction, was intact. A click preserved the scene for posterity and my report. "Do you know anything about demolitions?"

"No." The negative chorus sounded from both of my guys.

"Blowing things up is not in the grifters list of skills." Kevin noted ruefully.

"That's okay." I spun around and snapped their picture, catching them both in a candid photo. "I happen to have an acquaintance who knows something about bombs."

8

—·—

51 Across; 6 Letters
Clue: An authority
Answer: Expert

"What do you think?" I muttered the words in an aside to Kevin as I tossed the pasta salad. My gaze was focused on Rabi sitting at the kitchen table.

"Ducks, you've lost a few pieces over the side." A hint of reproach sounded in Mrs. C's tone.

Marcus laughed. "Kamikaze salad."

The boy was seated next to Rabi.

Monday evenings were usually not a group affair. Per our loose schedule that included game night or movie night later in the week, the early days left everyone on their own. The custom could be over-ridden for an on-going case, not to mention the stunning announcement concerning Marcus's adoption.

Kevin's homemade bacon cheeseburgers were the main course. Mrs. C had added her jacket fries. Basically, they're potatoes cut on the round like thick potato chips. Add her special seasoning salt then deep fry them. They're a treat.

I was tasked with tossing the salad. I expected points for my extra effort. Instead, a wrinkled hand tipped with purple polish blocked me with a ninja-like move.

"Please stop that." The older woman gently removed the utensils from my hand. "It's been tossed near to death, child. There's dressing on the utensils, the counter, and the floor. We're ready."

I looked around, stunned. I'd been focused on watching Rabi. A stone gargoyle would have given me more information than the former Special Ops veteran did. My confused gaze settled on my hubby. "I was going for effort."

"You have other things on your mind." He handed me a tray piled with toasted buns, sliced onions, mayonnaise, pickles, and tomatoes. "You did a wonderful job. Time to eat."

Marcus ran over to do his part. Together, we carried the food to the table. As we took our seats, Rabi set the camera aside.

Though I burned with a desire to hear his interpretation, I settled in while food was passed and plates were filled.

Rookie had taken up station lounging on a high stool set by the windows facing the street. Mr. Pickles strolled in, tail high in the air. His green eyes measured the distance to the counter top. He bunched his four white socks and his long legs beneath him.

"Don't even think it!" My raised voice startled the feline enough to pull his green gaze to me. "If either you or your sister put one overgrown paw on that kitchen counter, you and I are going to have it out."

His green gaze met mine with studied indifference. Then he tossed his tail in the air and marched into the living room to pounce on the new scratching tree.

"Don't act like you don't understand me." After yelling at the cat's tail, I scooted my chair closer to the table and fixed my son with a mock glare. "Look at me. I'm talking to a cat. This is your fault."

The answering round of laughter forced a smile to my face. The dinner discussion started with an update on our outing and the adoption, or possibly kidnapping of the cats.

"They're beauties, luv." Mrs. C's British lilt made the words sound like a purr. "What breed are they?"

Marcus made a slashing motion across his throat. "Don't ask."

"I don't know." I admitted with a chuckle. "I saw them drifting through the house. Lorelei wasn't big on discussing them. So of course, I kept asking questions about them. That way she couldn't talk about herself. One of Reilly's business acquaintances gave them to him out of the blue three years ago."

Kevin stabbed at the salad, making a tattoo rhythm on the plate. "Odd that a busy man like him would bother keeping a pair of kittens."

"He and Lorelei didn't care enough to get rid of them. The servants, a cook and a football fanatic, named them and fed them." So saying I bit into my perfectly cooked, juicy burger. I couldn't stop a groan of bliss. "This is ambrosia. I'm so lucky to have you."

"I know food is the way to your heart, Belden." Kevin accepted my compliment with a grin and a wink. "You're not wrong, but I'm lucky to have you, too."

Marcus slathered a jacket fry with ketchup, pausing before he took a bite. "Cats are very self-sufficient pets."

"They're here. Quit selling it."

"I looked them up on-line." Marcus kept on the conversation with his usual never say die attitude. "They're polydactyl. That means they have lots of toes. Regular cats have five toes on their front paws and four on the back. Rookie has seven on the front ones and five in the rear. Mr. Pickles has six toes all over. Twenty-four toes each. Cool, huh?"

Mrs. C stabbed a forkful of pasta salad. "Plainly, they are extraordinary cats. Just as you are an exemplary child and you'll soon be officially ours on the books."

Smiles and applause broke out again for the third time. Marcus high fived Rabi, again. We'd met Rabi and Mrs. C at the door with the unexpected good news. The entire Belden-Tanner Agency had gone through a second, possibly fourth, celebration – I'd lost count. Each outbreak came complete with yelling, dancing, hugging, more screaming. The whole bit.

From the yowling in the pet carriers, we definitely scared the cats right out of their fur coats. I only hoped they were having second thoughts about cozying up to the pair of handsome strangers who'd offered them free food, rich milk, and matching warm smiles.

"What are the available dates for the adoption ceremony?" Marcus eyed Kevin with a glowing face while smacking the table in rapid time. "We should decide now so everybody can plan."

Mrs. C's face broke into a gentle smile. "Oh, luv, I'll be there no matter the time or place."

Rabi's usual somber expression settled into an affectionate look. "Same."

Kevin swirled a jacket fry in the ketchup while he watched the scene. "The first date for the adoption ceremony is in four days, Friday, at thirteen-hundred."

"What a schmoozer." Despite my words, I couldn't hide my grin. "Using military time to get on the boy's good side."

Although tonight, no one in the apartment had a bad side. It was all sunshine.

"Waited long enough." Rabi snapped his fingers and pointed to Marcus. "Sooner's better."

Marcus pumped a fist. "Let's do it."

"I agree." I slapped the table. I still couldn't believe his adoption day was finally on the radar. My boy child had changed so much from the fleet-footed street urchin I'd chased four years ago. "As soon as possible."

We'd have a celebration later with my family. I'd already made plans for the five of us to go to Kentucky in June to have a second reception for my and Kevin's wedding. This would give us the opportunity to combine both our milestone events in one big bang. My parents had rejoiced to hear about the adoption. They'd already made Marcus part of the family.

Kevin covered my hand with his. He'd been with me and Marcus every day, working through every crisis, and helping gain a little boy's trust. My hubby squeezed my hand. "I'll text Mrs. Everett to confirm. We'll be there with bells on."

I clapped my hands. I couldn't help myself. Life was good, unless you were Thaddeus Reilly. My brain led me back to my murder case without warning. I toyed with the lettuce on my burger. "How soon can I shift the conversation to the case and still be considered a good mom?"

Marcus scoffed. "TR, you're the best. Everybody knows that, otherwise we wouldn't be here."

His tone was casual but that didn't stop the arrow cupid shot in my heart. I was borderline tears. I pressed my lips together.

Kevin raised his glass of water. "I agree. Here's to you, Belden and your penchant for picking up strays. Where would we be without you?"

As the others picked up their drinks, I lifted mine as well. I'd finally found a place I belonged. "We all found each other. To our family."

The glasses clinked. The drinks were drunk.

Now, back to the case.

Mrs. C gasped as she set down her glass. "You'll have another special day in your life, ducks. Your adoption day. You know what that means?"

That we weren't going to discuss the case right away?

My son smacked his glass hard enough to risk cracking it. "A party! We need to have an adoption party. We can invite Crawford and the whole gang, the people from the neighborhood, and the police."

The count was ticking up, but looking at Marcus's happy face I wasn't about to complain. We'd waited a long time for this day. I twined my fingers with Kevin's.

He met my smile with an affectionate look. "We'll pay the piper later. You're good at that."

Marcus was still wrapped up in the planning. "I can stay home Friday and go straight to the party that night."

Kevin cleared his throat. "You only get adopted once. Why don't the five of us go out to lunch before the ceremony? We'll do the big party Friday night. Then we'll sleep in Saturday."

"Yes!" The boy child threw his hands up in the air. "Two parties. Even better."

"Oohhh, could we invite the book club?" Mrs. C tapped the table. "Mrs. Smythe books reservations at the Astoria. We could get the Golden Ballroom. It has the connected patio with a view of the mountains at sunset. I've always wanted to have a grand affair at the Astoria."

We were officially in over our heads. My frugal instinct kicked in and put the brakes on my runaway enthusiasm. The Astoria was one of the priciest hotels in town mainly because their three ballrooms were in high demand as venues for weddings, black-tie parties, and political fundraisers.

Good thing those rooms were booked through the end of the year. "They can't possibly have an opening for Friday, that's only four days away."

The older woman shook her finger at me. "They had a last-minute cancellation just this morning. A bachelorette party got a bit out of hand. They kidnapped the groom and best man and eloped to Las Vegas

Sunday night. Most of the guests were at the Bellagio. So, they had an impromptu reception. The couple left for their honeymoon early."

I stared in amazement as my bank account screamed. "An elopement?"

Mrs. C reached out and tapped Marcus's hand. "Mrs. Smythe worried that it was too late to arrange another affair. I'm certain we can have the place for a song."

She ended on a triumphant note. Her raised brow followed by a conspiratorial wink to Rabi earned a nod and a smile from the quiet black man.

"Do it." Kevin squeezed my hand. "This is the only time we're going to adopt a son. Let's go big."

"Absolutely. It's worth it." My reservations popped like yesterday's balloon. My heart was about to burst from seeing Marcus's ecstatic expression. I nudged Mrs. C's arm. "Ask about the caterer. They may have the food already. Perhaps we could get a deal there, too."

Kevin smacked the table. "Good thinking, Belden."

"Excellent." Mrs. C beamed approval. She tapped her chin with the glittery blue tip of her fingernail. "I'll call an emergency meeting of the book club for tomorrow morning."

Her words called for a hard stop in my brain. "That's a thing for book clubs?"

"Definitely." Her British accent went even starchier. "We've had several."

I hated to have missed emergencies. "I never heard about them. Any details?"

Mrs. C looked a bit abashed. "Well, some of the subjects are rather touchy."

Kevin groaned. "Don't tell her that. She'll never quit asking questions."

I gave him my best mock glare before raising my glass. "Here's to the adoption party and the planner."

Again with the clinking of glasses.

With the glass of water at my lips, my mind once again turned to murder. How to get the discussion on track?

Marcus's laughter cut across my thoughts. "Rabi, you better tell her what you saw in the pictures. She'll either start to cry or she'll go ballistic."

The boy child leaned toward Kevin and put a hand in front of his mouth. "Smart money's on ballistic."

Kevin shot him a sideways glance and gave him a thumbs up.

I smiled at their banter and turned toward Rabi. Though Kevin and Rabi had briefly discussed the blast earlier, the pictures provided solid evidence. "So? What's your opinion of the explosion?"

"Professional." Rabi's drawl held his usual unarguable tone. "Directed blast."

"The living room." I stabbed a finger at him before turning to Mrs. C. "Did you see those pictures?"

As the older woman shook her head, Rabi flipped through the photos. He handed her the camera. Marcus peered over her shoulder.

"Nice one of you, luv." Her grin faded as she pressed her lips together. "The living room appears untouched."

"But the kitchen and the office above it were completely destroyed." I eyed the intact ceiling above us. "From the street, you wouldn't know anything happened. Part of the roof is even intact above the office."

Kevin leaned forward. "The blast blew out and up, not in a circle."

Rabi leaned his tall frame against the chair. "Debris field is directional. Narrow blast range."

"Up and out." Marcus leaned his chin against his fist. "Had to be the office he aimed to destroy. Not the kitchen."

Mrs. C dabbed her mouth with her napkin. Her green eyes narrowed in thought. "Then why not plant the bomb in the office?"

Silence reigned for several seconds.

I took advantage of the pause to make inroads into my scrumptious cheeseburger. The police can hunt for the killer. Lorelei can hope for salvation. I have my own priorities. It's not like I'd find the killer tonight.

Kevin snapped his fingers. "Lorelei was home. She heard him. Something triggered his suspicions. He couldn't risk going upstairs. He planted the bomb in the kitchen, knowing it would blow the office."

I swallowed a bite of jacket fry and raised a brow in Rabi's direction. "The bomb would have had to be designed to do the directional blast thing, right?"

He raised a forkful of the pasta salad and nodded right at me. "Directional is specialized. No last-minute change."

Mrs. C's frown multiplied the wrinkles on her face. "How does that help? The dead man was a nutter, eh?"

"It would be simpler if he was." I sipped my ice water to buy time. I tossed the clues back and forth trying to reconfigure my puzzle to fit, but... "I got nothing. Reilly could have removed anything from the house at any time. Why destroy his own office?"

The others studied me as they ate.

I glanced at Kevin. "Lorelei must be the X factor that kept him from going upstairs, but I can't see a reason why. He lived there."

"He didn't want to argue with her." Marcus pointed a ketchup-soaked jacket fry at me. "You said she always nags at you. He knew she'd start a fight, but he was on a deadline. If he planned to blow up his house, he meant to go somewhere else. Did he buy a plane ticket?"

Mrs. C stabbed her fork at Marcus with a quick thrust. "You're on to something, you are."

"I think he is." My son's question regarding Reilly's plans made me aware of how many basic avenues I'd failed to examine. In my defense, I'd had a full day so far. Was it still Monday? Would this day never end? "I'll have to check the airlines. He planted the bomb around midnight. It exploded at two-thirty in the morning. He would have had an alibi set up or an escape."

The new possibilities consumed me.

Kevin eyed Rabi. "What's the level of difficulty on a scale of one to ten?"

"Nine." The answer was immediate.

I steadied my hands on the table, struggling to digest the new information. "So, no casual construction worker could have done this? No, I read a how to on the internet?"

Rabi set his jaw and shook his head. "Military grade. Specialist trade for a civilian in demolitions. Weight bearing wall's intact."

"I didn't see that Reilly ever worked with explosives. He hires out. He had at least one ally." That fact should have been obvious from the beginning. Although in my defense a lot had happened since Lorelei's call. "We'll have to keep an eye out for experience with explosives."

Marcus's expression grew serious. "I'll go online and search for demolition experience or military service. I don't remember seeing anyone who knew about bombs and stuff."

"Thanks. Remember to check for a work history with mines or electrical experience." I tried to sound upbeat. Most of my brain was trying to unravel the main puzzle. "Reilly could have destroyed anything in the house at any time."

Marcus gathered his legs underneath him and knelt on his chair. "Did they kill him because he blew up his house?"

"There has to be more to the case than that." I raked both hands through my hair. "Am I going to have to solve the bombing before I can figure out the murder? Any luck on a copy of the will? Tiffany gave me the impression that she and the daughters profit."

Mrs. C's eyes lit up. Her whole body quivered with the force of the secret she was keeping. "Was she referring to the version filed last week? If not, it's no good, ducks."

I heard Marcus's "Oohhh", but my own surprise took over. My gaze remained on the older woman. "Lorelei said Reilly changed his will last month. He rewrote it again last week? Why would he make so many changes in such a short time?"

"Maybe he was on a deadline." Marcus burst out laughing at his own bad joke. "Get it? Deadline?"

When Kevin and Rabi joined in the merriment, I could only shake my head. As for the case, there were no answers to be had, of course. When the laughter died down, I continued with my questions. "Who gained in the latest version?"

Mrs. C grimaced. "Haven't nabbed a copy yet, have I? Tomorrow. It'll be there. Then we'll see who lost and who gained by the victim's death."

"Hopefully, Lorelei didn't profit from the new will." Good thing Crawford always gets a solid retainer up front. Our client might be in an orange jumpsuit by the end of the week, but at least we'll be paid.

9

— · —

31 Down; 7 Letters
Clue: Children or offspring
Answer: Progeny

Come Tuesday morning I was snuggled in my bed all nice and warm. I breathed a sigh of relief that I'd made it to dawn with no emergency phone calls. I usually woke up a few minutes before the six-thirty alarm went off. This interlude was my usual five more minutes under the covers before my day began.

When a jarring chime sounded, it took me a moment to realize it was my phone not the alarm. I groaned at the intrusion. This better not be Lorelei. I picked up the cell phone by feel and swiped the screen with my eyes closed. At least I was awake this time. "Hello?"

"Is this Tracy Belden?" A woman's hurried words slurred together softly in my ear. "I was given this number for a private investigator. I've lost something. I need it found immediately. When can you get started? Right now? I have a picture and a full description. Are you awake?"

I really wanted to tell her No. I'm thinking the "hello" should have given her a clue.

Instead, I struggled to a sitting position wondering if the woman intended to pause long enough for me to respond. "Take a breath, lady. I charge by the day not the hour. You're not on the clock yet."

"Is this Tracy Belden?" A desperate note laced through her voice. "I have to get started right away."

Kevin was sitting on the side of the bed. He looked over his shoulder, aiming a flat stare at me. "Would you tell your little friends to call at noon when I'm at work?"

I laughed silently as he smiled and blew me a kiss. Rubbing the sleep out of my eyes, I returned my attention to my caller as he walked to the bathroom. I needed coffee. "This is Trix— Tracy Belden. Who gave you my number?"

I was going to have words with someone. Right after I got some caffeine in my system.

"Detective Wilson. He's with the homicide department." Her hurried pace hadn't slowed down, nor had the anxious tone dimmed.

"Wilson?" My old buddy, the lead detective on the Reilly homicide. What had that man set me up for? The rat fink was going to owe me a plate of cheesy fries for this call. "Who is this and what exactly have you lost?"

"My name is Amy Reilly. I've lost a cat. I need it found and returned as soon as possible. It's very valuable."

A cat? That woke me up. I was going to kill Wilson. He gave out my number to look for a lost pet?

A wave of irritation stoked my temper, then the suspicion kicked in. Amy Reilly was the victim's younger daughter. Why was she worried about her father's cat? Amy had never lived in the Reilly mansion.

Why mention one cat and not the other? Did Amy know which cat she wanted?

I leaned against my pillows. "What's special about this cat?"

Silence greeted my question. I looked at the readout. The call was active. "Hello? Amy? Why do you want this cat found? Did Lorelei ask about it?"

Which I knew hadn't happened.

"How do you know Lorelei?" Accusation rang in her tone.

My brain sputtered. Talk about the right hand not knowing what the left hand was doing. "I was working for her before your father was murdered. After his death, she hired me to find his killer."

Stunned silence. Okay, it was dead air. I assumed the stunned part. This time I waited.

"Can you also work for me to find the cat?" A soft melodic tone imbued her voice with a hint of southern belle image. "She belonged to my father. I really want her back."

I tapped my finger against my lips as I noted her calculated attempt to play on my sympathy. Did she know there were two cats? Was it legal to double dip for an animal that was meowing outside my bedroom door? "How about we discuss it over coffee? Where are you staying?"

"At one of my father's condos." A breathy sigh of relief accompanied her words. "Penthouse floor in the Lucky Strike building."

Her father's offices were located in that building. He'd designed and built the structure years ago. The place still accounted for some of the most expensive real estate in town. Which for a resort town like Langsdale put them at a lofty level.

I signed off after agreeing to meet her at nine. No word of her older sister, Beverly, who was also staying in the building with her husband. When I first signed on to watch Thaddeus, I'd checked out his entire life. Marcus isn't the only one who can do research.

Moments later the intoxicating aroma of brewing coffee drew me into the kitchen. Rookie, the solid gray, twined herself around my legs, but I fought through.

Kevin was stirring a bowl of eggs when I took a drink from his cup on the way to getting my own. I gave him a kiss for his sacrifice.

He smiled ruefully. "I have to work today. The boss won't let me have it off."

I grimaced in sympathy, then gave him a wink. "You want me to talk to the guy? See what I can do?"

A leering look was his response. "He'd cave for you but I'd better put in the hours if I want to get paid."

I poured myself a cup full of coffee, inhaling the aroma. A variety of thumps and thuds from the loft bedroom proved Marcus was awake. I turned the sausage sizzling in the pan. "He seems oddly energetic for this early."

Kevin poured the eggs into the pan, adding salt and lemon pepper. "I gave him a heads up on your morning caller."

I laughed. "Way to motivate the boy child."

A moment later, Mrs. C let herself in at the same instant said child thundered downstairs.

By now I had the plates on the table so I was in perfect position to see him fling out his arm and point to me.

"Mrs. C," he said breathlessly. "T.R. got a call from Amy Reilly this morning. Meeting at nine o'clock with a possible murderer."

"Oh, good show." The older woman shot me a congratulatory look for my work in answering the phone.

I smiled, taking full credit for my hard-fought victory.

The boy met her in the middle of the room. "Detective Wilson gave Amy the phone number."

Mrs. C's expression clouded over with a frown. "That's rather playing in the rough, giving out your private number. I can't say I approve."

"Thank you." I agreed wholeheartedly. "I don't like it either and I'm going to have a few words with that man."

"Rabi's pulled up on the street." The other woman trundled into the kitchen on her pink slippers. "Ought to wait on the details, so as not to repeat."

Another judgment that won my approval. I brought the sausage to the table. Marcus made toast. Kevin loaded the plates with cheesy scrambled eggs mixed with diced onions. Rabi sauntered in. By the time we'd eaten everyone knew the scant information I'd learned. We'd also tossed the same questions back and forth.

Marcus's frown looked permanent. "You're not giving them to her, are you?"

"She only said she wants one back. She may not know there are two animals. I doubt they're mentioned in the will. Failing that, Lorelei owns the cats." I hadn't figured out Amy's angle. It might be a ploy for information but she'd seemed truly clueless that I was investigating her father's murder. "I can't believe Amy wants either of them. She's desperate for something. I just have to find out what."

The boy stabbed a bite of egg. His face clouded over before clearing quickly. "Mrs. C, what are you doing today? Can you stay here and watch the cats? They might be lonely when everyone leaves."

"They've been raised by servants in a mostly empty house." Anyone listening would have thought we were talking about neglected children.

"Of course, luv." The British lilt to her tone seemed to multiply her sympathy.

I might as well talk to the wind. Both of them ignored my comment.

Mrs. C continued blithely on. "I'd no plans but a possible nap later. The book club isn't until Thursday. I could do a few loads of laundry here while I wait, can't I?"

The woman doesn't mind doing laundry. Who knew people like that existed? I jumped in quickly. "We can't be too careful with the cats, and feel free to do as much laundry as you'd like."

Kevin eyed me with an amused look at my transparent and guilt free flip-flop.

Marcus pointed his fork at her. "Keep the door locked unless it's us."

The boy was far more worried about cat-nappers than I was.

"No one is taking those cats." Kevin assured him in a stern tone. He sounded fully ready to go to battle to keep the animals. "Not after I hauled fifty pounds of felines up the stairs and bought revolving litter pans. They're part of the family now."

His reasons sounded convincing enough on the surface. However, I had to wonder if Kevin saw in Marcus another lonely young boy, one whose grifter family had no time for anything but the almighty dollar.

Kevin's family of international grifters, the Feilens, have pulled off some of the most audacious scams in the world. However, their adherence to the bottom line demands absolute loyalty to the cause.

A Feilen joins the business the day they're born. Each member is on the clock until the day they die. A lack of focus is not tolerated.

Anything or anyone that fails to contribute to the scams is not tolerated. This includes pets. The price for this single-minded determination is morality, humanity, and the man sitting at my table defending a pair of adopted, possibly stolen felines.

The thoughts rolled through my mind as the tension in Marcus's shoulders eased.

"Good." The boy breathed a sigh of relief.

Evidently feelings were running high. I raised my mug of coffee in a show of solidarity. I have to admit my action was more out of loyalty to my son and husband than affection for the cats. "No animals are leaving this house."

Rookie chose that moment to stretch her long legs across my lap and put her head on my thigh. She spread out her paws. She had huge feet, seven toes on each paw.

I stroked her polydactyl toes as I counted them. What could I do but pet her? Then, of course, she started purring like a living massage wrap. I could get used to this.

While I wasn't convinced her fur was non-shedding, it was amazingly soft and silky. I met her pleading green gaze. Great, I was being played by a cat. I stroked her spine and took a long drink of coffee. "I'll work on the handyman books for a bit, then I'll talk to Amy and find out if she knows which cat she's looking for and why."

***

I was early to the appointment. That gave me time to chat up the doorman as well as the woman at the front desk of the building. We bonded over adopting children. Her brother had adopted two sisters from Guatemala.

My new buddy Wanda confirmed that Reilly spent a good portion of his time in this building. Between his company offices on the tenth floor and his constant traveling, he couldn't have spent much time at his house. Hence Lorelei's surprise that her husband had rushed home early from an out-of-town business meeting. The actions didn't fit the man's profile

The story of Thaddeus Reilly according to Wanda could have come straight out of a press release. Nice guy. Great boss. Generous to his employees. Everybody loved him.

Until early yesterday morning when someone didn't.

That's when I remembered to ask about Brandon Haigh. Wanda only knew what Marcus had already told me about Haigh and Reilly fighting at the council meeting. No one in the building had a clue why the Drake was such a flash point for either man.

Wanda reared up out of her chair. "Mr. Reilly was certain Brandon set the fires that damaged the Drake. Now it's set to be demolished. So, Brandon won in the end."

Except Reilly was dead. "Is Brandon Haigh in the gallery today? Do you know?"

The other woman shook her head. "Not this week now that you mention it. He always comes in with a smoothie and waves hello."

Coincidence that the man hadn't kept to his routine after a dead body turned up? Like cops, I didn't like coincidences in my investigations.

On the matter of the murder, most of the fingers in the building pointed at the wife, my client. The consensus on the daughters was middle of the road. Good workers. Nice that they came back to the business. It made Reilly very happy.

That's when I rode the express elevator straight to the top. It was nice. No stops. The doors opened to a private alcove in front of the penthouse door.

When I knocked, the door opened almost immediately.

A pixie-sized young woman stared at me. Her violet-colored eyes were framed with dark eye makeup. She had straight, flat-black hair that hung almost to her waist. "Ms. Belden?"

"Yes." I stepped forward as she waved me in.

"I'm Amy Reilly." As she spoke, she gasped and stepped in to block my path. "Do you have any ID? I have to check."

"Sure." I reached into my purse and pulled out my flip wallet. I felt a sense of déjà vu as I remembered Marcus had done the exact same thing by the Reilly house. I hid a smile as I showed her my P.I. license. "Good enough?"

The license could have been my library card for all the attention she gave it. Evidently, checking for a possibly fake P.I. sneaking into the penthouse hadn't been her idea.

She shrugged and moved out of my way, waving me forward. When clinking plates sounded from the next room, she spun on her heel. Thrusting herself into my personal space, her wide eyes stared up at me from only inches away.

I reared back and stopped for the second time. I honestly thought she was going to plant a kiss on my cheek. My initial reaction was to tell her she also wasn't my type.

Instead of stopping, she moved closer, putting her lips next to my ear. "My sister and brother-in-law didn't leave as usual. I told them this meeting was your idea. Don't mention the cat."

This information was delivered in the same rapid-fire breathless tone as her initial call. She swiveled on her heel with a dancer's grace and – third time's a charm – she waved me in.

Keeping a neutral expression in place, I logged the secret cat business and walked into a spacious living room. A one-and-a-half floor atrium gave a feeling of openness. The cream-colored walls and a block of windows that flowed from the floor to the ceiling took my breath away.

As an architect, Reilly knew his business.

Amy caught up with me. She motioned to the open archway, flanked by large ferns on either side. "Ms. Belden is here."

"Did you check her ID?" The overly patient tone was solidly in the big sister camp.

As the tired sigh and annoyed look could only come from a younger sibling. "Yes, I checked. No one is pretending to be her."

I couldn't think of anyone who *wanted* to be me.

We walked into an equally light and airy sitting room, kitchen combination done in a pearly translucent green.

Beverly, four inches taller than her sister and aided by three-inch heels, looked me directly in my eyes. Dressed in a professionally tailored black suit, she appeared the consummate business woman. She held out her hand. "Ms. Belden, I've read of your previous cases. I'm confident you'll find who murdered our father."

"That's my intention." I released her hand after a quick shake. "Thank you for taking the time to meet with me. The sooner I get the details behind your father's actions the sooner I'll be able to make progress in the case."

"Of course." Beverly took charge as Amy retreated to sit at an island nearer to the kitchen side of the room. The older sister gestured to the glass topped table with a brass pedestal base. "This is my husband, Jeremy Newcomb."

The man at the table looked up with a distracted air. Slightly rounded shoulders, he stood an even six-foot. Blond wavy hair, brown eyes, regular features.

He was also a world class jewelry designer. He sold and commissioned to the top boutiques and clients in the world. He'd been on the ladder to success when he met and married Beverly ten years ago in New York City.

From what I remembered they both loved the big city life. Jeremy had made no secret about his unhappiness regarding their move to Langsdale.

My initial research when this was a divorce case hadn't been in-depth on the children. I'd only done a cursory amount of background. I had no idea what stick or carrot Reilly had used to get his daughters to uproot their lives. From what I'd learned, he hadn't been supporting either in their previous careers.

If he'd used threats to bring them back and hold them, their anger might account for his violent death at the time, not three years later.

"Would you like some coffee, Ms. Belden?" Jeremy asked.

"I'd love some. Thank you." Smiling in thanks, I took a seat at the table. "Call me Tracy, all of you."

"Oh, good." Beverly's tone lost its formal air as she sat to her husband's left. "I have a lot to do today and I'd like to get this interview over with as soon as possible. We'll do anything we can do to assist you, Ms. Bel—Tracy. I want my father's killer found so we can move on."

"Speaking of moving on," I took a steaming cup of coffee from Jeremy, adding a nod of gratitude. "Are you? Staying with the company? Staying in Langsdale? Returning to New York City? You and Jeremy have maintained your condo there."

"You're direct. I like that." She raised her brows as she saluted me with her cup. After meeting her husband's gaze, she faced me. "I've decided to stay with the company my father built. It's a world class business. I'm not the architect my father was, but he and I have recruited top talent. Surprisingly, he mentored a handful of the most promising architects in the past few years. The company is well positioned for the future. Jeremy and I can work anywhere."

Her polite expression never changed. Her gaze stayed on mine.

If I didn't know better, I could almost believe coming to Langsdale had been her idea from the beginning. Good thing I'd never had to play poker with this woman.

A smile that bordered on a sneer touched her husband's lips. "New York City here we come."

His relief was patent from his relaxed tone to the light in his eyes. He didn't bother looking up. His smiling gaze remained locked on a graph sheet where he sketched a linked chain with hanging baubles.

Beverly's expression remained businesslike. "What did you want to know?"

I let the warmth of the coffee seep into my hand as I kept my professional mask in place. "I know you've been over this with the police but I need to go over some basics."

I couldn't go through with it. "You know what? Let's not bother."

I'd planned to jump through the hoops and follow the script, but why? Crawford had gotten the story from the cops. I knew the alibis and timelines for the daughters. Beverly and husband in the condo together. Both asleep. Neither left all night.

I love alibis that involve sleep. If they were conked out, how could either of them swear what the other was doing? The obvious alternative is that they were in it together. Equally plausible.

Amy was out with six friends at a gallery exhibit. Then, the entire group went drinking and dancing until three o'clock in the morning.

On the surface, they were both solid alibis, but not air-tight. Who couldn't slip away from a bunch of drunks in a bar full of dancers?

My instinct said that neither young woman had pounded their father's skull in with a blunt object. But I wasn't writing anyone off the suspect list, including my client.

This conversation needed a live hand grenade. "Were you aware your father filed a new will last week? Did he mention changes to your inheritance regarding the company?"

Beverly jerked as if she'd taken an arrow to the heart. "How did you know...?"

She stared at me for a heartbeat before she collected herself. "You're good. Was that a shot in the dark?"

I weighed my answer. "I've been watching your father for a week. I did my research. On the surface, he presented himself as a generous, caring boss and friend. But to get ahead in this business he had to have the personality of a tank. He was determined to succeed and look like a hero doing it. I have it on the word of a world class profiler..."

Don't look at me like that. Kevin is the best in the business. I'd put my hubby's skills against any profiler the FBI has to offer.

"Being the ultimate good guy was one way of getting people to admire him." The last bit were my words, but that's what people on a power trip do. "He liked being on top of the mountain."

The woman's mouth curled to a sneer. "You have him pegged. Few people recognized that side of him."

Jeremy's jaw tensed, though he didn't look up from his drawing. Introverted and quiet, the man would never have understood Reilly's attitude. No doubt the father and son-in-law had their share of run-ins.

Beverly continued. Her gaze remained even and unmoved. She'd had a lifetime to deal with her father's personality. "He'd threatened to change his will before the end of the month. He said he'd leave Amy and me with nothing if we didn't sign a contract swearing never to leave the business."

My jaw dropped. I didn't try to hide my surprise. Reilly hadn't struck me as a family man. "He all but ignored you and your sister for most of your lives."

Beverly's eyes flamed with the light of battle. No doubt she was her father's daughter. Those two surely butted heads. "I told him he couldn't control our lives anymore. He could keep his company and his money. I wasn't going to waste my time fighting his demands. As you said, it was a game to him. I assumed it was a bluff."

So she said. I shook my head. "He filed the new will last week. I don't have the details yet."

Her shoulders remained squared but relaxed. "I left an executive position in the banking industry when I came here. If I'm out, I can get a job in New York City by Friday. I told him the same thing."

"What about you, Amy?" I tossed the question over my shoulder as I spun to face her. "Staying or going?"

The younger woman gave an unladylike snort. "I've been in PR creating schlock about the company. I planned to leave as soon as they put him in the ground and the police lift their lockdown order. But the stage plays and the acting opportunities in this town are as good as San Francisco with frankly, less competition. I'll split my time."

I'd expected Amy to hit the road once the case was solved. I swiveled in the chair to face Beverly.

"I also like being close to Aunt Tiffany." A cloud passed over Amy's face.

Several clues clicked into place like an old-style pinball machine racking up points. The unsteady gait, the drawn, tired face. "Is it cancer?"

Beverly's eyes widened. She regained her composure but a new wariness settled in her gaze. After a moment, she nodded. "Yes."

"I'm sorry." It was hard to pivot from that to their father's murder, but I had little choice. "Is that how your father got you here? Or was it another case of the carrot or the stick? I'm thinking the latter. He didn't like to lose."

A sharp intake of breath sounded from Amy. My peripheral vision caught a sudden move as Jeremy's head jerked up. My attention remained on Beverly.

Did none of them give me credit for having any skill in investigating? The cases were puzzles with a limited number of possible answers. I was good at puzzles. I was obsessed with solving puzzles once I started them.

A small smile of admiration touched Beverly's mouth. She pressed her fingers against the edge of the table. "The stick definitely."

"What was his threat?" I asked.

She leaned against her chair. "He swore he'd destroy my reputation in the business world if I didn't quit and join his company. He also threatened to undermine Jeremy's business. He'd have pulled out all the stops to have his way. As you've noted, he didn't like to lose. I had no choice."

"You must have been furious. I would've have been." I sipped my coffee as she responded with a fatalistic shrug. "You and Amy had been living your own lives. Your mother died fifteen years ago. You were a senior in high school. Amy was a freshman. Your father had no real connection with you since then. Tiffany took care of you. Why did he force you back?"

My gaze swept around to include Amy who twined a lock of hair around her finger. She stared at me with wide eyes. "He threatened to close any play I signed on with. He never explained himself to me."

I faced her sister.

Beverly's mask fell. A frown wrinkled her forehead. "My father's motto was: Never explain or apologize. It makes you look weak. And yes, I asked for his reasons from day one. I never received an answer of any kind, satisfying or not."

No help there. I sipped my coffee as I thought of the options. "Chronic illness? Dying man?"

Beverly shook her head. "He had to complete physicals for insurance for a number of contracts we signed with him as the chief architect. He either faked the results every year or he was healthy."

Jeremy snorted, still focused on his design. "That old man was strong as a horse. Unfortunately."

I tapped the side of my mug. "Corruption? Leave you and Amy holding the bag?"

Beverly's answering chuckle held a note of evil. "My condition for coming on board was that he open the books to me. The accounting department was moved to my division. I told him from day one that if he ever set me up, I'd put him in jail or I'd put him in the ground. He knew I wasn't bluffing."

Considering her father was dead, the woman wasn't shy about her threats.

She stabbed the table with her finger. "This company is clean and legit. The police have been through the books. You can look at them if you want."

"I don't want." I also didn't have the skill or the time. Besides, as Reilly's sister had noted, the man had built his company up from nothing. The business had wealth and prestige, which all came back to him. He wasn't the type to risk his baby or his reputation. He also had no reason.

I muddled around searching for another angle as my crossword puzzle re-sorted the black-and-white blocks. The man counted money as success. How could he make more money? Where do you go from the top? "Did he ever mention diversification? Did he invest in any other companies?"

Beverly drew away as if struck. Caught unawares, she simply shrugged.

We turned as one to face her husband. He blinked several times before snorting in disbelief. "You're kidding, right?"

Beverly chuckled.

I kept my gaze on him. Answering a question with a question is an easy way to avoid a truthful response. I know. I use that ploy all the time. "Have you ever heard anything about your father-in-law buying into another company?"

Jeremy met my gaze squarely. "No, I have not. I don't care about Reilly's wealth. Never have. I use precious metals and flawless stones and gems in creating my jewelry. Reilly was only concerned with looking good. He was a fake, a liar, and a user. I won't pretend I'm sorry he's dead. I hope his killer is never caught."

Succinctly put. I turned to Amy. "You?"

She gave me her wide-eyed pixie gaze, which I was beginning to trust less than her sister's poker face. The younger woman looked clueless. "I wasn't at the executive level. I never heard about Dad getting involved in another business. He wouldn't trust anyone else with his money."

Unfortunately, that was a judgment I tended to believe. Reilly had been up to something, but what? "Any ideas why he would blow up his own house?"

Jeremy shook his pencil without looking up.

I took it for a no, but it might have been "leave me alone."

Amy shrugged. She looked equal parts of bored and impatient. "He loved that house more than he loved us."

Beverly threw up her hands.

One more unanswerable question in a long line.

"Do you think Lorelei killed your father?" I prompted, hoping to put the fox in the henhouse.

This time the older sister shrugged. "I wouldn't blame her if she did. He was a difficult man to live with and she can be volatile. She admits to hitting him over the head. According to the police, her story fits the timeline. The police found his car on the street by the house. I don't know why he didn't park in his garage."

All neat and tidy. Why didn't those answers satisfy me? I looked at Amy, quiet through the interview. "Did you get along with Lorelei?"

Amy chuckled. "She didn't pretend to be something she wasn't. Dad got what he deserved when he married her. Before Dad forced me to return to Langsdale, I only saw her at the wedding. I've seen very little of her since. I don't move in her circles."

"Same here." Beverly interjected. "Other than business dinners or society affairs, they lived separate lives. I'm thirty-three. Lorelei is only a few years older. She was our father's wife, not our stepmother."

"It would be easier if she killed him." Amy's eyes lit up. "Then this would be over."

Not for Lorelei.

The younger woman's expression was hopeful rather than vindictive, but she was an actress after all. "I'm not sure why she would attack him. Perhaps he confronted her with evidence of an affair. She'd lose a lot in a divorce."

Lorelei's hysteria on that first telephone call could have been the raw emotion from killing Reilly. Her words might have been an honest confession, one she later regretted. There was no outside evidence to support her version of confronting him by the pool and hitting him with the bat.

I found myself nodding, in agreement and admiration. "I'm sure the police have thought of that possibility. I did, that's why she and all of you are still on the suspect list until either the police or I find absolute proof who killed your father."

Bev gave a rueful laugh.

"You all had reason to hate him." I continued. "Bev and Jeremy could be covering for each other. Your alibi is a bunch of drunks in a crowded dance bar."

Sure, I was deflecting. Mainly because I hadn't eliminated anyone. I know Lorelei could be playing me. Kevin might be wrong in his assessment of her. We're not perfect. But the widow was the only person who'd hired a P.I. to find the killer.

I stared into my lukewarm coffee. "Okay, thank you for your time. If I have any other questions, I'll contact you."

Jeremy flipped his notebook shut and shot to his feet.

Beverly and Amy stood as well.

I walked slowly toward the front door. How did Amy intend to get me alone?

Beverly shot past me with Jeremy a length ahead of her. She glanced over her shoulder. "Lock up, honey, will you?"

Her husband was already in the hall. He punched the button as she continued to speak. "We have plans for dinner. We'll see you when we see you."

"Okay." Amy answered from a foot behind me. "Bye, guys."

I was still headed toward the door when the elevator closed on the other two. "No, don't wait for me. I'll get the next one."

"They're very in tune with each other." Amy touched my arm. When I stopped, she walked past me and shut the door. "Wow! You really know your stuff. You were like a real P.I. asking those questions."

"Gee, thanks." Did these people think I just walked in off the street? Though I get a bit embarrassed when people gush about the handful of high-profile cases I've solved, Amy had gone to the opposite corner. I took a calming breath. What did I care about this clueless pixie? "About this missing cat."

"Yes!" She clapped her hands. Putting a hand on my shoulder, she turned me around. "Let's sit by the window. It's way more relaxed. I can't stand that high-pressure stuff Beverly does. You're good at it."

"Thanks." I think. I sat in a tan and white chair in a compact sitting area.

My gaze followed the straight lines of the city streets. The mostly low-profile buildings and the bright colors that dotted certain clusters made an eye-catching mosaic on the landscape. The golden glow of the desert sand under the sun was a picturesque contrast to the chain of purple mountains in the distance.

Amy took the seat opposite. She clasped her hands on her knees. "Have you found the cat?"

"I had to get my son to school this morning." Which was true but neatly side-stepped the fact that I had to step over the cat when I left my apartment. "I also need more information before I search for a cat. How can I confirm I have the correct cat? Is it a purebred? Or a special breed?"

She cocked her head to one side. "It's a big gray cat."

My expression remained serious. If only Kevin and Marcus were around to hear this description. "Do you have a picture? Is it related to your father's cat that Lorelei mentioned to me?"

Both of her hands shot forward. She stabbed the air frantically until she nearly poked me in the eye more than once. "That's the cat."

I grabbed her wrists and pulled her hands down. This woman had no concept of personal space. "Have you asked Lorelei? It's her pet."

Amy scoffed and pulled away. She flipped her hair over her shoulder with a sharp gesture. "That woman doesn't care about anything but herself. She said the cat got out the night my father died. That's all she knows."

"I thought there were two cats." I noted innocently. "I saw them drifting through the house when I met Lorelei for my first case with her."

"Two, hunh?" She turned a blank expression toward me while she tapped her lip. "You may be correct."

Yep, two. Put money on it. Talk about not caring. I'd only been in the house three times. Amy had lived in town for three years. From now on I planned to call Mr. Pickles and Rookie rescue cats. "Why is this cat important?"

"The friends who gave Dad the kittens lost their two females." Her tone was relaxed. She met my gaze directly. "They caught a contagious disease. They want this one back to breed. They're willing to pay to find her. Will you help?"

She was either a better liar than I'd given her credit for or she believed this story. "Who gave them to your father?"

"Paul and Brooke Findlay. Paul Findlay is Dad's accountant. They met in college or right after. I'm not sure which." She rattled off the facts without pausing to think. "I've been friends with their son, Chad, since we were young. They got the cats from some friends who breed the animals."

I followed her rambling chain of connections while holding onto the Findlay thread. Paul's name had popped up on some articles on my original research. I'd planned to interview him regarding the murder. As an accountant to a wealthy dead man, Findlay was definitely a suspect.

On the surface, the story was just dumb enough to be believable. The main flaw was that no one cared enough to find out that Rookie couldn't have kittens.

"I've never looked for a lost cat, but I could make some calls." Usually, I insist on getting paid whether I'm successful or not. That seemed a bit much considering I had possession of both felines and I had no intention of giving either of Marcus's new pets to any of these people.

Amy clapped her hands. "The Findlays will be thrilled."

"I'll do my best." I walked to the door. I wasn't sure I was farther ahead. I not only had the same questions I'd come in with I had a new one. Why was someone looking for a cat none of them cared about?

10

— • —

54 Across; 8 Letters

Clue: A point where two or more things are joined

Answer: Junction

I stared at the old-fashioned floor dial above the elevator as the indicator climbed toward me. My responsible brain prompted me that Findlay Enterprises was on the sixth floor.

My irresponsible half rejected doing the right thing, so did my gut. To be fair, I was still dragging from yesterday and my puzzle was frozen in place. I had too many questions. Nothing made sense.

Although this would be the best time to find out whether the Findlays knew they were worried about this lost feline.

The elevator ding was like a wake-up call. I was on a case. I had to do the right thing. Time to find out how the Findlays were taking the news of Reilly's murder.

When I stepped onto the elevator, my thoughts drifted to Kevin's progress at our latest handyman job. I told my finger to press six, but when the elevator hit the third floor I realized I was aimed at the lobby.

My heart did a happy dance. I was tired. So, I gave in. I could work on my handyman business and give my brain some time off. I'd talk to the Findlays after lunch. Hitting speed dial for my hubby, I smiled as the floors zoomed by.

At the sound of Kevin's hello, I started talking. "How about I do some paperwork and billing for B&T Inc, then you can have lunch with your wife?"

"I'd love to." His words came with a heavy sigh. "But the drywall for the Copper Mine Pavilion was delivered early. It's sitting poolside where the cement mixer has to park to pour the new pool at one o'clock. We're going to have to work straight through to get it installed. No lunch until two at least."

"Do you have the manpower?" The elevator doors opened onto the main lobby. I walked out and stood beside a lush fern. "I can call around."

Kevin's voice grew distant as he shouted an order at someone. "I got a hold of Jimbo. He and Nathan, still together I might add, came to help."

I had to smile. "Okay, you were right about them. I'm glad it worked."

He chuckled and continued his litany. "I called Rabi. He said they were overstaffed. His manager let him take a few days of vacation. I think the guy had to agree or Rabi would quit, but it works for me."

"Marcus will be thrilled." Rabi had taken time off and worked for B&T Inc. several times over the past few months. He'd commented more than once about taking early retirement and signing on with us. A job change our boy child was heartily in favor of. "Our son doesn't like the constraints of Rabi having a nine-to-five job."

More voices sounded over the phone line.

"You're busy. I'll talk to you later. Love you." I signed off and told my heart to forget about seeing Kevin. At least I could walk around the block to clear my mind. I passed the front desk, aiming a polite smile at Wanda, the woman I'd pumped for information earlier. When I waved farewell, her eyes lit up. Her hand flipped convulsively in a come-hither gesture.

The grin on her face widened as I approached. She glanced around the quiet lobby with a furtive air, leaning close as I reached the counter. "She's here."

I had no idea who this woman was talking about. The obvious answer was to fake it. "I never expected that to happen."

"I know. Right after you'd been asking about her." The receptionist fisted her hands as if we'd caught someone in a trap. "She went to the eighth floor. I watched the elevator readout. That's the floor for Mr. Reilly's attorney."

"That sounds interesting." I truly was intrigued, but I was also clueless.

My buddy put a hand on my arm. "She was alone. Mr. Findlay wasn't with her."

Brooke Findlay. Of the missing cat. The news re-ignited my puzzle solving fire. I shoved any thought of escaping to the back of my brain.

I fought to keep the shock off my face as a bolt of adrenaline shot through me. "How long ago did you say?"

"I didn't." The security woman straightened, pulling her hand away as a delivery man pulling a dolly walked up escorted by the doorman. She pointed to the hall. "It's okay, Ralph. He can go through. They're expecting him."

After nodding to the doorman who exited, my buddy tracked the guy to the corner while she scanned the lobby. "She took the elevator up fifteen minutes ago. She'll see Nelson Robach. Reilly's personal attorney since he started his company. The old guy's a tortoise. One speed: super slow. No way you'll pass her coming down if you go up now."

"I owe you a special brew." I slapped the desk. I started to walk away then stopped. Fishing in my purse, I slipped a ten-dollar bill on her desk. "Treat yourself."

While waiting for the elevator, I texted Kevin. "Got a lead on B. Findlay."

My nerves jingled as I watched the floors flash by inside the elevator. The dead man's attorney, the accountant's wife, a changed will. What did Brooke or Paul know? Were the Findlays in for a windfall?

I ground my teeth in frustration. If only I had the details of the new will. Perhaps by now, I could get the information. When the doors slid apart, I exited on the eighth floor behind two men in business suits.

The thick pile carpet, shiny wood paneling, and gold framed land-scaped paintings gave clear notice of wealthy lawyers with high-dollar clients. As did the receptionist at the front desk, blocking easy access.

I hid behind the twosome and did a quick u-turn toward the re-strooms. A quick recon showed the sitting room and stalls were deserted. My thumb hit the quick dial for my favorite Brit.

"Hello, ducks." Her lilt sounded in my ear. "What's on the go, eh?"

"The will." I took a seat at a comfortable chair and spun around to face the mirror. An elegant love seat with pretty pillows and two individual stations with mirrors completed the posh design for the sitting area. After spinning in a circle, I eyed the door. "Do you have any details on Reilly's changes, by chance?"

"I'm *that* glad you called." A faint scuffing sounded over the phone line. "Let me top off me tea and I'll give you the grit."

I could only hope it would be quick.

A chair screeched as she dragged it out from the table. "Me friend and I had a long coze this morning, didn't we? Heard all about the family. You don't care about that."

"Not right now," I admitted. "I'll be happy to listen later."

"Only one change to the will." The older woman's tone overflowed with barely suppressed excitement. "Older daughter still gets the company. No motive there."

Reilly's threat had been bluff, just as Beverly had said. I wasn't surprised.

"Younger daughter has a fair bucket of cash to start anew."

I tapped my chin, still trying to get a feel for Reilly. "He knew what drove his daughters. He took care of them at the last. They'll both be wealthy women. But for all they knew, he could have cut them out of his will."

"Hmmm." The older woman sipped her tea noisily. "Could come down to timing."

If they believed he'd cut them out. Did anyone know he'd changed his will? "What update did he make?"

"An addendum." The clear clang of a teaspoon tapping on her china cup rang in the air. "It gives Lorelei a huge cash settlement in case of Thaddeus Reilly's death."

My breath whooshed out of me as if I'd been punched in the gut. That was the last thing I wanted to hear. "Lorelei profits from his death?"

"Aye." A note of excitement mixed with the dread in the woman's tone. "What do you make of that saucer-full? Puts another nail in your client's coffin I'd say."

"So would I." I spun the chair around in a slow motion. "Lorelei had no way of knowing what change he made. She honestly believed he was filing for divorce."

Not that the police would believe she didn't know she'd inherit. I chewed my thumbnail. "Any idea how much she'll get?"

"Could be a farthing. Could be a fortune. As my mum used to say." Mrs. C's voice carried a breezy air. "Can't get to the details. That would be illegal."

I stared at the phone in astonishment. Who was I talking to? Since when have we drawn the line at the law?

"My source didn't have the amount, but it's a goodly sum."

There you go. I opened my mouth to respond, but Mrs. C cut me off.

"There was mention of a briefcase with a special security measure to unlock the contents. Odd bit, that. Have the police opened the case they found in Mr. Reilly's trunk?" She sounded very put out. The woman loves to be in the know. "Not long on details, but Mr. Findlay is purported to have the answer. I've got naught."

I made a sympathetic noise and signed off. I aimed my feet at the young man at the front desk. A frontal assault. Identified myself. Flashed my license and my smile. "I'm a detective working on Mr. Reilly's murder. I need to speak with Mr. Nelson Robach."

After a quick check on his computer, he pointed through the glass door. Mr. Robach's inner sanctum proved to be guarded by a stern, competent looking soul. Sylvia O'Brien met my explanation with a sympathetic expression but no give. "Mr. Robach is with a client at the moment. If you'd care to leave your card, I can have him contact you or I can make an appointment for you."

I leaned on her counter. "How long will he be busy? I have some time. I could wait."

Her professional mask didn't falter. "His schedule is booked for the next hour."

She hadn't bothered checking the schedule. She only had one executive to track. However, an entire hour to meet with Brooke? That was major business or he had another client coming.

I hadn't expected to gain entrance. Information was the key. "I can't stay that long. Here's my card. Please have him call me when he's free."

Turning on my heel, I walked to the elevator like I had all the time in the world. Inside I was counting the seconds. From my earlier research, I knew Findlay Enterprises had offices on six.

Mr. Paul Findlay might be in his office. This would be a perfect time to ambush the man who tracked Reilly's finances. Perhaps Findlay had helped himself to some of the dead man's fortune. That would make a juicy motive.

Means? Reilly's head was bashed in. A handy rock?

Opportunity? I had no idea where Paul or Brooke Findlay claimed to have been at the time of the murder. Probably not asleep the way this case was going.

My Tuesday had been a busy day so far and I was still working on the basics in my crossword puzzle.

Police: Where were you from midnight to two o'clock on Monday morning?

Any normal person: Sleeping.

It was a reasonable alibi. It was my alibi. Fortunately, I didn't need one. Paul Findlay did, and I was willing to bet he hadn't been in bed.

The thoughts whirled through my brain on the short ride to the sixth floor. No one blocked my access to the offices here. There was a glass door covering one end of the hall that read Findlay Enterprises.

Inside, I marched toward the front desk. "I have an appointment with Mr. Findlay. I'm late. I know. Parking was crazy. I'll go through."

Confusion reigned on the poor woman's face. "Wait. What? Whoa."

This was totally my style. I was well past her at the first word. By the time she was on her feet, yelling the ubiquitous: "You can't go in there." I was turning the knob.

The man inside the office was seated behind a large desk. He was backlit by the panel of windows behind him. Sunlight shone on the papers laid out before him. His concentration had already hit a stopping point if the frown on his face was any indication.

"Paul!" The woman rushed up behind me. "She swept past me without stopping. She's unbelievably rude."

Not the worst thing I've been accused of.

"I'll call security and have her removed."

Not the first time that's been threatened.

I kept my gaze fixed on Findlay. "I'm Tracy Belden, a private investigator looking into the murder of Thaddeus Reilly. I'd like a bit of your time to clear up a few facts."

Reilly and I agreed on one thing. I rarely apologize or explain. Those options have never advanced my cause. State the facts and take what comes. As long as I was moving forward, I was good.

Except when security actually did throw me out, which has happened more than once. I go for the gamble.

Findlay studied me for a moment. He tossed aside the pencil he'd been tapping. "No, Irene. I'll speak with the young lady. Thank you."

Irene hissed between her clenched teeth. Her intense gaze could have burned a hole through me. With a final growl, she spun on her heel and stormed out, shutting the door behind her.

Findlay gave me a rueful look. He was a big guy. He had move of a paunch than Reilly had cultivated and his hair was thinning, but Findlay was roughly the same height and build. "Is this the way you usually meet new people? By bursting in on them?"

"It works more often than you'd think and I'm not a patient person." Why lie? Best to come clean. "I play the odds. Sometimes I lose, but I'm here."

He crossed his arms, leaning some weight on his elbows. "Who are you working for?"

"Lorelei."

His brows raised to his thinning hair. "She and Thaddeus had their share of troubles recently."

Yet Reilly hadn't filed for divorce, and he hadn't shown Lorelei proof of her own indiscretion. He'd conducted an affair that put the aces in his wife's hands, especially given his obsession with his public image.

For a shrewd, self-made man, Reilly's actions made no sense. Everything about him said he would never risk his company, but his actions put a share of the business within Lorelei's grasp.

Reilly must have had a plan, but I had no idea what his end-goal could have been. Certainly not his own murder.

"Lorelei had a few cards of her own to play." Including pictures of Reilly with his current lover. Findlay and I were getting along so nicely. I decided to wait before launching that fireball. "The Reillys' possible divorce is not why I'm here. His murder is. Where were you between eleven p.m. and three a.m. when Thaddeus was killed?"

He leaned forward a touch too casually. His gaze remained frozen on mine.

The M.E. said death occurred between midnight and six. I'd gone with eleven to pad the spread. I wasn't sure who Reilly's ally had been, but he and Findlay went back a long way.

Greed could make enemies of allies or friends. The gang and I watched *The Treasure of the Sierra Madre* a few weeks ago. Spoiler alert: everyone turns on everyone else to get the treasure. They all end up dead. Destroyed by greed.

Had Paul Findlay's greed caused Reilly's death?

Findlay played a game of stare down for several seconds before he caved. "I was working until eleven-twenty."

"Those are late hours for a Sunday night. Is that usual?"

"I had to go over some papers before Monday morning."

"What then?"

"I stopped to get gas then I grabbed a few items at the Blue Miner's Market. I got home around twelve-thirty."

How extensive was his shopping list? He lived ten minutes from this office building.

His mouth creased in a sardonic grin. Evidently, he'd read my skepticism, or the police had tagged him for the same reason. "I took my time at the store. Destressing after a long day. You can check the receipts or the grocer's security camera. I'm certain the police have a copy by now."

I doubted Wilson would share. Although the man deserved to have his chain yanked after sending me a case involving a lost cat. If the detective didn't cooperate, Crawford would be able to confirm the times. Or I had my own contacts I could exploit.

I ran a hand through my hair, hoping to stimulate my brain cells. "So, you have an alibi for part of the time of the murder. When was the last time you spoke to Reilly or met with him?"

Findlay threw down his pencil. A closed look hid his thoughts. "I've met Mr. Reilly several times over the past month. He had several business matters to attend to."

I kept my expression neutral as my interest flared.

Reilly had been up to something. If not divorce, what? In the last week, he'd altered his will then he'd blown up his house. He had a co-conspirator. Findlay was his associate. If anyone knew what the scam was, odds were on Findlay.

I pressed my point home. "I'm sure you know all of his secrets. He's been your client for decades. You have an interest in his success. I'm beginning to wonder if you gained more by your association than you should have."

He rose to his feet in a sudden move. His solid frame, complete with a basketball-sized belly hanging over his belt, made an over-sized silhouette against the bright sunlight outside the windows.

"I don't like what you're implying, Ms. Belden." Findlay walked toward me. The dark shadows covering his face masked his expression. "You would be wise not to repeat your theories in public."

The light behind him shifted as he walked toward me. Sad, weary wrinkles creased the skin around his eyes as they met mine. "I'm not at liberty to discuss Mr. Reilly's business with you. Time for you to leave."

So endeth the interview. A moment later, I found myself once more standing in front of the elevator. While he hadn't laid a hand on me, I knew when someone meant business. I had no intention of tangling with Mr. Findlay.

It was finally lunchtime. I was worn out from talking to these people. Hopefully, no more leads would land in my lap in the next hour. Too bad I was on my own for lunch.

As I crossed the lobby my gaze rested on my buddy at the main desk. The woman was on the phone as she directed two young people to a side corridor.

Without warning my feet turned in her direction. A question about Findlay's alibi had found its way to my mental list.

She greeted me with a smile reserved for co-conspirators. "Did you get any new information for your case?"

"I did. Thank you, it was a great lead." My smile was genuine. Meeting people face-to-face is the only way to truly get an impression of them. As Pop always said, "Looking isn't enough. You have to ride a horse to get a feel for the beast."

The now empty lobby gave me a perfect opening. I leaned on the counter. "Do you keep a record of people entering and leaving after hours?"

"Absolutely." She glanced around as her hands opened a drawer on the desk. A light gleamed in her eyes. "You want to check Mr. Findlay's exit time the night of the murder? I thought you might. The police took a copy."

Her voice lowered to a conspiratorial whisper. She planted the book in front of me. It was already open to the correct day.

Sure enough. Paul Findlay, four-thirty p.m. entry. Exit: eleven-twenty-two p.m. Seven hours. The color of the ink on the time was different from the signature.

I pointed at the line. "Who writes in the time?"

"We do." She pointed to herself. "The employees only sign their name."

"Do you know who was here when he arrived or left?" I don't suppose she worked the weekend.

Wanda nodded. "I saw him come in. I was working extra hours for a buddy."

"Anything seem off that day?" I was taking shots in the dark. Sometimes they hit the target. Sometimes they don't. "Did he look tense? Act differently?"

She shook her head. She frowned at her apparent lack of information. "He didn't want to work on Sunday. Who does? I was picking up overtime and he was on deadline. He was wearing the hat and scarf with his company's logo, as usual."

When she chuckled, I asked for details.

"His wife ordered tan hats and light weight neck scarves with their logo in March as an end-of-quarter present for the employees. I have one somewhere. Mr. Findlay has worn them every day since they arrived."

"Hmmmm." Interesting, but not helpful. "He didn't leave for lunch or dinner?"

Wanda shook her head. "He must have had something stashed in the fridge in the office."

I filed away the information and waved goodbye. However, my brain refused to mark the question resolved. Something about his alibi gnawed at me.

Wilson owed me. Might as well take out my frustration on him. Perhaps I could get a look at that security footage.

I had to find a way to punch a hole in Findlay's alibi.

If I didn't make progress soon, Lorelei might be trading in her designer dresses for a prison jumpsuit.

11

—.—

9 Across; 6 Letters

Clue: Passionate to an excessive degree

Answer: Fervid

Wilson wouldn't answer my phone calls and didn't respond to my texts. I stopped by the police station but he was out on a possible homicide.

That stopped me cold. A *possible* homicide?

I shouldn't have asked.

Two bidders at a high-brow art gallery came to blows over a small Van Gogh. When the auctioneer called out the going, going, gone routine, the losing bidder jumped the other guy.

I could add that alcohol had been served freely, but I'm certain the brawl would have happened if they'd both been stone cold sober.

In the end, the man who started the fight got smacked with a Chinese bronze from the auction items. The police were called. Ambulances came. The victim was mistakenly reported DOA and Wilson was called. When the detective arrived at the hospital, turned out the guy was still breathing. The other bidder was patched up and arrested.

I had a mental image of Wilson waiting by the guy's bedside like a vulture, waiting for him to kick off.

The auction house issued a statement that the auction would continue tomorrow at the same time.

Why let publicity go to waste?

I listened to the details while thinking about my next step. I hope the guy recovered, but I had my own problems.

Once outside the police station the spring sunshine cleared my head. If you can't answer a puzzle clue, move on to the next one.

I wasn't ready to face off with Brooke Findlay about Reilly. That left Brandon Haigh, the gallery owner.

No one at the gallery in Reilly's building had seen or heard from Haigh in days. They refused to give me any contact information for him.

Fortunately, Marcus's printouts included a secondary address buried in the records, a small rebuilt warehouse.

If Langsdale had a worrisome neighborhood, Haigh's other location qualified. I made sure to lock up my Buick, but no car thief is desperate enough to steal my fifteen-year-old heap.

Seeing the warehouse in daylight left me wondering why the city powers let this decrepit building stand. The roof was sagging. Colorful graffiti marred two sides of the place. Several windows had boards over them. Kevin and I could have done a better job of patching with a weekend's worth of work.

The front of the building showed no sign of life or habitation. After checking the address, I parked behind and walked up a set of six cement steps cracked with age.

The metal door had no bell or intercom. I decided to save my hand from pounding. A quick search provided a metal pipe. An ear-splitting banging of what felt like an eternity left me with ringing ears and trembling arms.

I paused to catch my breath, ready to concede defeat. My latest failure did nothing to improve my mood. Leaning on the pipe like a cane, I pondered returning to my day job at B&T Inc. There was always paperwork to fill out, e-mails to answer, and supplies to order.

The door jerked open without warning.

Gasping in surprise, I picked up the pipe and stepped back.

"What's your problem, lady?" A black guy in his thirties with the square build of a wrestler yelled in my face. "You trying to knock down what's left of this rat hole?"

I swallowed my heart and considered my response. Brandon Haigh was a lanky, forty-eight-year-old white man with dark brown hair. Who was this guy?

I was still catching my breath when the man gestured at the pipe I'd shifted to my shoulder like a baseball bat.

"Who are you going to slug with that thing?"

I tossed the pipe behind me. "I'm Tracy Belden, a private investigator looking into Thaddeus Reilly's murder."

The man's expression didn't change one iota. He didn't blink an eye or breathe hard.

"Bully for you." His gaze raked me over as his snarky tone echoed into the large room behind him.

How clueless could this guy be? Reilly's murder had been the top story for two days. Langsdale wasn't so big that the story could be lost in the shuffle.

I took a deep breath, gathered my thoughts, and reached for my license.

The guy retreated into the building. He grabbed the door and started to shut it. "What are you going for?"

Jumpy, or what? I held out my hand. "I'm getting my P.I. license."

I slowly pulled out my holder and held it up. I felt like Marcus.

The guy stepped forward. Once he'd examined it in the light, he handed it back.

"I'm Tracy Belden, just like it says." I slipped the license into my bag. "I'm looking for Brandon Haigh. He's not at the gallery or his apartment. He evidently hasn't been around for a few days. Do you know where he is?"

The man's face melted into worry lines. "I wish I did."

"I need to speak with him regarding a case. We might both benefit if you give me some information, perhaps I can help find him."

His icy expression thawed. After a moment, he stepped aside and waved me in with an expansive gesture. "Anything you can do will be great. I'm really worried about him."

"Progress." I muttered as I crossed the threshold. He didn't bother to ask who I was working for or why I was here, and I didn't offer. We'd get to that in time. "By the way, what's your name?"

"Wayne Scovell." He closed the metal door with a loud clang and threw home the bolt. "Do you like espresso?"

"Sure. If you put enough water in to make it real coffee."

He answered my smile with a roaring laugh.

I walked ahead of him into a large open room. Wooden packing crates lined the walls. Plastic covered canvases were piled on crates and wooden sawhorses that had planks laid across them to serve as a tabletop. Bright paint showed through the coverings. Smaller cardboard boxes were on the floor. Handwriting on the boxes listed the contents as ceramics, jewelry, hangings.

The main area was well lit from the high windows and the tall work lamps. However, opaque plastic tarps blocked off large side rooms.

I ventured closer to a tarp, stepping between two tables. At the last minute, I glanced down to check the contents of an open box.

That's when I saw the tripwire. My brain screamed, but my foot was already in motion. My body seized. The wire went taut. As my heart went into adrenaline over-drive, the string snapped.

My peripheral vision caught movement on my left. I turned to see an eye-level object hurtling toward me. I threw my body down and back, but the round ball aimed at my head was too close.

A yell sounded behind me.

In the blur of the moment, someone, something hit me. The motion wrenched me sideways and threw me to the floor.

Wayne's muscular body landed on me with plenty of momentum behind him. The air whooshed out of my lungs. My head and hip hit the cement floor with a jarring explosion of pain. Stars flickered in my brain and before my eyes.

The pressure lessened as Wayne rolled off of me. His face loomed before my eyes. His mouth moved below his worried eyes. Noise hit my eardrum loud enough to make me wince, but my brain couldn't decipher the words.

He raised his head and yelled at someone I couldn't see. I may have blacked out for a few seconds. The next thing I knew I had a pillow cushioning my head and a cold rag on my forehead.

Wayne was kneeling next to me, taking my pulse. "Medic, National Guard."

Evidently my skepticism showed on my face. I tried to smile.

"Stay still."

His warning was pointless. I couldn't tell if my smile muscles were working. I was certain the rest of my body wouldn't.

The fast beat of running footsteps skidded to a stop next to my ear. The upside-down face of a young female loomed over me. Her hair looked light brown but most of it was hidden under the backward facing baseball hat. Her thin, pale face was tense with worry. "Is she dead? Tell me she's not dead. I'm sorry."

The piercing tone stabbed into my brain like six-inch nails.

"Shhhh!" Wayne managed to keep the command low-pitched and threatening at the same time. He grabbed something out of the female's coveralls. "Annie, be quiet."

Wayne snapped on the penlight he'd confiscated and did a quick wrist flipping check of my eyes. "Your reactions are good. I don't think you have a concussion, but you should be checked. Can you contact someone to drive you home? If not, I will."

"No, to both." When he opened his mouth, I realized I'd spoken aloud instead of just thinking my response. "Help me sit up. Then get me some aspirin and the coffee you promised."

I pushed myself to a sitting position. The stars in front of my eyes were gone. The headache had receded a bit. I took a deep breath and gave Wayne a go-ahead nod. He put his arm around my shoulders and helped me to my feet.

"I'm sorry. So, so sorry." Annie whispered a string of apologies as she grabbed my elbow on the other side. She came up to my shoulder. "On the bright side, the booby traps worked. The instructions on the internet were spot on."

"Oh, goody." My snarky tone made her wince. I followed it up with a glare. "Did your instructions specify the... what? Five-pound weight?"

She bit her lip and nodded.

I pointed at the ball, pulling the twine tight. "That could kill someone if it connected with their skull. It could have killed me. I don't think you'd do well in prison. If you insist on setting traps, use a weighted beanbag and aim it at the gut."

That's what my brothers had done in years gone by.

Annie blanched at the implications. She pulled away in time for Wayne to walk me to a sawhorse table with napkins and paperwork on it.

The man fixed Annie with a hard stare. "I told you not to use that heavy of a weight."

The young woman clasped her hands in a white-knuckled grip. "I wanted to follow the instructions exactly the first time. I'll switch the weight out."

She scurried away without looking back.

The tantalizing aroma of fresh ground coffee brewing filled the air. I inhaled and let the smell fill my senses. "Fresh ground beans are the best. I applaud you."

"Thank you." He went through the motions of flipping switches and watching gears spin. A short time later, he set a mug of steaming coffee and three aspirin in front of me. "The best coffee in the house."

I popped the pills and washed them down with a long sip of the hot brew. When the brew hit my bloodstream, I sighed in satisfaction. "Now, Wayne, we need to talk business."

He winced at my sharp tone. "I need a cup of espresso."

While he refilled the machine, I hit him with what little I knew. "Brandon Haigh has been pushing to have the Drake building destroyed to make way for the new plaza. Why does he care so much?"

Wayne fiddled with gadgets and buttons and knobs. The machine whirred and spat forth a stream of dark liquid, filling the air with a rich aroma.

I pointed at him. "Start talking."

He took a seat opposite me and met my gaze. "I don't know."

Wayne's expression settled into a weary frown.

I waited for a long minute, but he simply stared into his cup. "I expected more."

"So, did I." He muttered as he ran a hand through his hair. "Annie and I have worked at the Haigh Galleria for years. I was with Brandon since he opened the place. Two years ago, his parents died within weeks of each other. Ever since he went through their house, he's been a man on a mission."

"What's his mission?" I asked.

The man threw his hands up in the air. "He kept going on about how he found his brother's Blackberry. There were notes in it about a crime."

I struggled not to grimace. The last thing I needed was yet another crime to investigate, but I had to ask. "What crime?"

He stroked his steaming cup with one thumb. "His older half-brother, Lester Jensen, embezzled two hundred fifty thousand dollars from the Dawson Architectural Firm twenty-five years ago. Then, he ran off. He's never been found."

Dawson. Reilly had worked for that company right out of college. I took a sip of the delicious brew. "Did Brandon think his brother was innocent?"

"Yes and no." Wayne dismissed the thought with a sharp gesture. "Evidently, the evidence was overwhelming. Brandon admitted Lester took money for a fifty-thousand-dollar balloon payment on his parents' house."

Annie quietly returned to the main room, slipping out from behind a tarp.

The embezzlement seemed straightforward enough. "And Lester stole the extra two hundred thousand as a bonus for his troubles?"

Wayne winced. "Brandon didn't think so. He and his parents never believed Lester would take the additional money and leave them without a word. Brandon swore Lester planned to payback the fifty thousand."

A fuzzy picture was fighting to take form. I needed more background. "What does this story have to do with the Drake?"

"Timing." Wayne's fist hit the table in rapid succession with slow, steady thumps before stopping. "After he found his brother's stuff, Brandon researched everything he could find about when the Drake was built."

I held up a hand to stop his monologue. I knew when the building had gone up. I'd seen the answer in multiple stories in the media. "That's when his brother disappeared?"

"Exactly," Wayne confirmed. "Lester stole the building funds. There were just pouring the foundation when he took off."

Oh, boy. Wayne spoke in a matter-of-fact tone, with no change of expression. Although, I was keeping a neutral mask on, too. Perhaps he saw the same picture that was forming in my fevered brain.

Missing money. A missing man. A fresh foundation. To me those clues pointed in a very bad direction. Brandon evidently thought so, too.

Wayne continued without pause. "Once Brandon completed the research, he became obsessed with the plaza project. He was determined to put the project where the Drake now stands."

Except Haigh didn't care about the plaza. He only cared about demolishing the Drake. I tapped my lips. "He never said why?"

Wayne's jaw tightened. A darkness crept into his eyes. "Not in so many words. He said nothing could be done without evidence."

Evidence. Of another murder? Such as a skeleton in the cement? "His parents died two years ago. A few months later he started crossing swords with Thaddeus Reilly."

The man looked at me directly. "Brandon spearheaded every effort to ensure the plaza would be built where the Drake stands now. Reilly fought against that location from day one."

Twenty-twenty hindsight can't be beat. Neither can preplanning. Eighteen months ago, Reilly had started traveling more, working more, and possibly stashing money with his accountant's help. Reilly hadn't been planning to divorce Lorelei. He'd planned to leave before his past crime would be uncovered. "Did Brandon know anything about explosives?"

"Brandon grew up around them." Wayne frowned, evidently surprised at the change of subject, but he answered without hesitation. "He put himself through school working with his father who was a demolition expert in a silver mine."

"Mines specialize in directed explosions." Such as the one that destroyed Reilly's house. A slow rolling epiphany added a bullet point to Haigh's profile, but where did that fact get me? Why would Haigh blow up the house? Revenge?

Wayne's narrowed gaze met mine. "Who are you working for?"

Took him long enough to ask, but the guy was desperate to find his boss. "I'm trying to find Reilly's killer."

"Wait." Wayne flung his arm out, pointing to a wall. "You think he blew up Reilly's house? Why would he?"

That's where my chain of logic crumbled. "I don't know why anyone would blow it up."

Especially Reilly, who was seen planting the bomb.

"The wife wanted to destroy evidence of wrongdoing." Annie piped up with the answer right away. Her expression remained eager and unsuspecting.

I splayed my fingers across the rough wooden surface of the makeshift table and struggled to keep my tone even. "Lorelei was in the house when the bomb was set to go off. Besides, she or Reilly could have destroyed any evidence in the house whenever they wanted."

Wayne reached over the table and clinked his tiny cup to my mug. "That's why you're the detective."

Recognition at last. I'd convinced Amy Reilly and Wayne Scovell of my abilities. I basked in the glow akin to a lit match. Now if I could only make progress. "When was the last time you saw Brandon Haigh?"

Annie leaned against the counter, a disappointed look on her young face. "Saturday afternoon about four. He rushed into his office. When he left an hour later, he didn't even say hi or bye."

Sadness followed by resignation flashed across Wayne's face. "Brandon was especially agitated this week. I saw him leave the gallery Saturday as well. He hasn't returned any calls or texts since then."

Late Saturday afternoon. The timing worked. Did Haigh realize Reilly was planning to bolt?

Haigh might have murdered Reilly during an argument. The repeated blows could have been fueled by rage over his brother's alleged murder. That scenario would wrap the matter up rather nicely. Haigh as the murderer meant the police had to find him. Lorelei would be off the hook and I would be done with her for the second time.

At first glance, Haigh as the killer sounded solid. Except my theory didn't complete my crossword puzzle. I cursed under my breath. "Do you think Haigh killed Reilly and took off?"

Wayne slammed both fists on the sawhorse. "If Brandon killed Reilly, he'd be dancing on the street corner taking credit. No way would he take off and leave unanswered questions."

"Like his brother," I noted.

"Exactly." The whispered voice belonged to Annie. She looked at me with soulful eyes. "Brandon swore if he disappeared to count him dead."

"He wouldn't walk out on us." Wayne slumped, putting his elbows on the table. "What should we do? I don't want to get Brandon in trouble, but we may be in over our heads."

On that point, I agreed wholeheartedly. "Dismantle the booby traps and call the police. In that order."

Annie took a deep breath. Rebellion was written in the gleam in her eyes.

"Not a word." I added steel to my tone as I stabbed my finger at the young woman. "Reilly was murdered. Your boss threatened him and may have started several fires. That's arson."

The outrage bled out of her face with each stroke I painted. She clasped her hands. "Do you think he's dead?"

I tried to copy Kevin's sincerity. "I don't know."

I heaved a sigh and stood. "Call the police. Tell them everything. Ask for Wilson. Tell him Tracy Belden sent you."

That last shot brought a smile to my lips. Served him right.

Wayne nodded as he headed toward the door with me. "What are you going to do?"

"I'm going to try to incriminate another suspect." Which meant getting a look at that tape of Findlay at the convenience store if I had to stake out Wilson's house all night.

12

— · —

23 Down; 9 Letters
Clue: Showing no signs of life; lifeless
Answer: Inanimate

Late Tuesday evening, as the sun sank behind the mountains, the valiant members of the Belden-Tanner Detective Agency retired to their spacious headquarters.

"That's how you begin a detective report to your boss." Marcus extended his arm and dropped an imaginary pen, which seemed odd since he'd been typing on his laptop. "Erle Stanley Gardner would be proud."

"I'm sure he would." I gazed around our open living room which led to our not so roomy kitchen. "Headquarters, you say?"

Kevin clapped his hands. "I like it."

Of course, Mrs. C and Rabi added their approval as well.

"Mmm-hmmm." I was vastly outnumbered in the fight for sanity in this household. Instead of a win, I settled for pointing to my son's laptop. "That paragraph is not going into my official report."

"I already filed it," Marcus crowed. "Boom."

I tried to glare at the boy, but I was distracted by the feline behind him.

Mr. Pickles had draped his long body across the back of the sofa. His paws dangled on each of Marcus's shoulders. The feline looked like a curved, gray neck pillow, except for the green eyes.

Rookie was sitting between the boy child and Rabi. Her erect stance reminded me of the hieroglyphics in Egyptian tombs. She stared at me through slitted eyes while Rabi stroked her fur.

That's all the boy needed, feline allies against me.

A chuckle escaped my lips. "This is how Crawford knows I don't fill out all my reports."

Kevin eyed me through narrowed lids. "Sure. *That* paragraph is why."

"Getting back to business." Since I couldn't win this argument. I pointed at the boy child. "What did you learn about Reilly's finances around the time the Drake was built?"

A light gleamed in Marcus's gaze. "The Drake was the first piece of real estate Reilly invested in. After interning with the company during college, the Dawson Firm hired him and gave him the chance to buy in on the ground floor. The cost?"

Pausing for impact, he spread his arms wide.

Mr. Pickles leaned forward as if he were waiting for the revelations.

"Two hundred thousand dollars. Also, none of his close relatives died around that time. Where would a twenty-five-year-old guy get that much money?"

Mrs. C's knitting needles shot into over-drive. "There you have it, eh? The missing money from the embezzlement."

"I checked into Jensen's case." Marcus put a hand over his shoulder to stroke the gray feline. "He paid the balloon payment like Haigh said, no other cash ever turned up that could be tied to Jensen."

"It's circumstantial but it all fits." Most importantly, this would explain Reilly's actions over the past two years and his insistence that the

Drake not be demolished. "I like the Haigh angle. Having the gallery guy as the killer would solve my problem and my case."

Mrs. C sat on the end of the sectional, several inches beyond the reach of my curled legs. "Once the police track the man, we'll have an idea of when he left town."

"If he left town." Marcus imbued the words with a threatening tone. "I think Reilly killed him and buried the body underneath the hedges. Only to be found by the co-conspirator. That's when Reilly was murdered and became the second victim."

I was used to his flights of fancy, but his theories were usually based on the facts. "There's no grave in the common area behind those houses. The police would have found it. Haigh is alive."

Kevin clicked his tongue. "I seem to remember your last South of France theory ended up with us finding a body."

That was during my first solo investigation, when my missing woman case turned into murder.

With Wayne and Annie's worried faces in my mind's eye I honestly hoped a second body wasn't in the offing. "Please. One body in this case is enough. If Haigh's not the killer, I'm back at square one. I honestly don't know who murdered the man."

Marcus had added the information on Haigh and the Findlays to the whiteboard earlier. I'd stared at the information time and again over the course of the evening. One more review didn't bring enlightenment. I threw myself against the sectional.

Kevin, Rabi, and Mrs. C had varying expressions of sympathy for my obvious frustration.

Marcus caught a piece of popcorn in his mouth as he followed my gaze to the board. "You did a lot of stuff today. Good job."

His show of sympathy brought a smile to my lips. "Thanks."

Kevin and I had spoken the same words of encouragement to him many times over the past few years.

"I didn't meet Brooke Findlay in person. There's no telling whether Paul would share Reilly's financial plans with her." I struggled to add confidence to my voice, but I was annoyed with myself. "Until the police confirm Haigh's whereabouts, I'll continue investigating the others."

Mrs. C looked up from her knitting. "That Inspector Wilson cleared Mrs. Findlay, didn't he?"

Marcus looked over the laptop with a frown. "Most of the suspects have been cleared. That means one or all of them are lying."

"You got problems, Belden." Kevin's hands slapped a rapid beat on his thighs. "No luck getting the Findlay tape?"

My smile broadened. "No luck *seeing* it. I finally tracked down Wilson and made my wish clear."

Confronting Wilson at the police station on my second attempt had been one of my few victories. Our clash at the end of my day provided a bright spot to a frustrating series of interviews. A noisy confrontation. A mutual yelling match. Blame and accusations on both sides.

Turns out the bidder from the auction survived. However, Wilson had to spend his entire afternoon interviewing Wayne Scovell and Annie, whose last name I now realized I never bothered to find out.

That's a hole in the next report.

However, Wilson was facing an entire evening of paperwork.

The only thing I learned was that I'd lost another suspect. "Meeting with him was the most satisfying part of my day until he said Brooke Findlay had an alibi. Multiple witnesses swear she was at a dinner for politicians in Las Vegas."

Kevin looked over at me. "Were we the only people asleep during the murder?"

"Us, Tiffany Sweet, and the Newcombs, if you believe their story." I stared at the board. "It's like everyone knew Reilly was going to get killed and they made sure they were seen somewhere."

Marcus's frown covered his entire face. "That's your guess? Everyone did it?"

I sat up straighter on the sectional. "They knew ahead of time. Everyone had an alibi."

Marcus looked at the others. "She's losing it. That's sad."

Kevin chuckled. "Have faith. She'll bring it home in the end."

I wasn't so sure. The clues from the dark corners of my mind were aligning. "And then there's the cat."

Rookie and Mr. Pickles stared complacently from their new positions atop their multi-level scratching tree. They'd followed the entire debate with their big green eyes. What role did the gray female play in this puzzle?

"Arrrghhh!" I clenched my fists toward the sky. "I almost had something. Now all I can think of is a cat I can't find."

Rabi raised a brow and pointed at the gray beasts. "You looking?"

"For answers." I spat out the words even as I smiled at his joke. "Why do they want the cat? Kevin took them to the vet. There's no chip in either of them. They have no secret pockets. They had nothing on them."

Marcus cocked his head to one side. "Rookie had the collar."

I felt my face go slack. Shock coursed through me. "What collar?"

The boy child drew back. His dark eyes turned to Kevin.

My hubby slapped a hand on his forehead. He had a horrified expression on his face. "Oh, no."

My eyes widened as my man walked to the front closet. How many times had I ranted about why anyone would want this cat?

Despite my outrage, curiosity overrode my irritation.

Besides, how could I blame a man who'd gotten up with me in the middle of the night? He'd faced down a bomb followed by police questioning. By the time we rescued the cats, Kevin had been awake for fourteen hours with only a three-hour nap.

I took a deep breath as rustling noises sounded inside the front closet. It would be wonderful if he came up with some clue in this blank canvas of a case. "These are both indoor cats. They never had collars."

Marcus held out both hands, palms up. "Rookie did yesterday. It was squeezing her neck like she was going to choke. You were busy taking pictures of the house. Kevin got it off her."

Kevin returned like a warm, disgruntled wind. His look of disgust was aimed inward. "I put it in my jacket pocket and wiped it from my mind."

"I can't imagine why." As I caught the prize in my cupped palms, I waved away his regret. "A phone call in the night. A bomb. Police. A dead body. It was a long day by six o'clock in the morning. All that matters is I have a clue now."

"That's no cat collar I've ever seen." Mrs. C stared intently at the metal... collar? "Looks like a bracelet, doesn't it?"

"Yes, it does." Geographic lines in red and yellow metal covered the flat gray surface. At random intervals on the metal threads small gems glittered in the light. Emeralds. Rubies. Sapphires. There was no pattern. I stretched the slim band between my hands. Holding it out to my hubby, I pointed at the bling. "Are these real?"

"No." His quick judgment all but walked over my question.

Mrs. C chortled from the other side of the room. "Of course, not, luv."

What did I know? I was blinded by shiny things. Not so blinded that I would miss an opening for more information. Time to call Lorelei. I picked up my phone with one hand while I toyed with the bracelet in the other.

My client picked up on the first ring. "Hello?"

"Lorelei, how did you know a cat got out the night you called me?"

A moment of silence allowed the ring of glasses clinking and a murmur that brought to mind fine dining. "I don't know. Wait. I saw a sparkle, a reflection of moonlight on the collar."

"Your cats never wore collars when I saw them." Silence greeted my comeback. I waited for several heartbeats. Murmured voices sounded. Lorelei asked for a blue dress in another size without flowers. I gritted my teeth and decided to try another track. "I found it by the way."

"What did you find?" Her voice was distant and distracted. "I'd like the shoes to match."

"The cat and the collar." I answered, putting her on speaker and pulling the phone away from my ear. "Do you want them?"

"What do I care about those animals?" Irritation warred with impatience in her voice. "The housekeeper and the cook named them and kept them. Take the cats to an animal shelter and get back to business. I need to go to New York to buy a wardrobe as a grieving widow. My designer has a new line and I can't leave town until the police arrest someone who is not me. I'm paying you to look for my husband's killer."

Some people are so picky. "I'll keep the cats as a bonus. I'm working on finding the murderer in my spare time."

Marcus pumped both fists in the air as he listened to Lorelei's complete indifference to the fate of the felines.

My client disconnected without a farewell. The more I stared at the bracelet the more the lines seemed to be on the verge of forming a pattern. I dialed another number. "Hey, Amy. I have a lead on the missing cat."

The noise coming over the line was much more raucous this time. I moved the phone away from my ear not bothering to put the pixie-sized actress on speaker.

"Good for you."

I rolled my eyes at her slurred words. This one was not the brains behind any part of this scheme. Or she was an incredible actress. "Do you have Brooke Findlay's number? Isn't she the one who wanted the cat?"

"Oh, sure." She rattled off a phone number and hung up without a goodbye.

"So much for her being involved in intrigue." I dialed a third number. Putting the phone between my head and shoulder I used both hands to flip the stretchy bracelet inside out. Perhaps I was missing something. At first glance, the silver hued metal held no secrets that I could see, just the normal hinges connecting the different pieces.

Brooke answered on the first ring.

I gave her the same story I'd given Amy.

"You found her!"

Her screech lanced through my eardrum like a knife. I dropped the phone to massage my ear.

Kevin put an arm around my shoulder. From the interested looks on the faces around the room, it was obvious Brooke's reaction had carried.

I switched the phone to my ear with an intact eardrum. Then I decided to play it safe and hold it in front of my face. The woman was still babbling away. I didn't bother waiting. "I have a lead on the missing cat at an animal shelter on the south side. It's five miles from the house. No telling where she's been, but she's big with extra toes on each paw."

"That's her! Is she okay?" Her voice shook. "Her collar and tags were still with her?"

I grinned and waved the collar in the air. Brooke was the only one to mention the collar.

Marcus gave me a thumbs up. His dark, gleaming eyes reflected my smile of satisfaction.

I flipped the bracelet to the back side again. Stretching it in and out only proved there was nothing hidden or taped between the sections. However, I had one card left to play with Brooke. "She has a long scratch on her neck. Not deep. No stitches and no collar. But she's okay. You ready for the address?"

The screen blanked before I said okay. I just couldn't stop my mouth from uttering the last question. I showed my phone to Marcus who'd been hanging on every syllable. "She didn't even say goodbye."

Marcus grinned. "Rude."

A giggle sounded from Mrs. C. "You can kiss your extra bobs good-bye, eh?"

That drew a chuckle from everyone plus a grin from Rabi.

"It's not the first time I've shot myself in the foot." I set the phone down to focus on the bracelet. The inner metallic side caught my attention. I expanded it as far as I could. "There are symbols on each of these sections. They're not matched correctly. How did you get this apart?"

Kevin reached out. His quick fingers pointed to a pair of catches that held the bracelet together.

Laid out flat, the piece of jewelry was six to seven inches long. When I stretched it out to check the connections, it was nearly ten inches. "Don't we have a set of tiny screwdrivers?"

My son pointed at me. "I bought those. I told you we'd need them."

We had an entire collection of surveillance equipment any detective would envy. "And you were right."

Rabi was on his feet. "I'll get them."

Taking the sections apart took five minutes. I spread them out on the coffee table. Marcus sorted them while I finished. Working together, the boy and I matched A to A and B to B and so on in under five minutes. Add a bit more time for reassembly and we were done.

"There you have it." I held up the flat piece and studied the lettered side. "What did that gain us?"

"Oy." Mrs. C sat up on the edge of the sofa. She twirled her knitting needle in a circle. "Flip it, luv."

Of course, the jeweled side with the design. I turned it over only to find myself blinking in surprise. The random pattern of lines and jewels now formed a stylistic yet distinct pattern.

"That looks familiar." Marcus leaned in. "That's an electric current. We learned about it last week."

I stretched the bracelet out and in. "Why design a thing like this? There has to be a reason."

My son was typing furiously on his phone. "I'll show you the picture."

How would that help? I spread my hands out. "I believe you."

"Connect the ends." Rabi's low drawl imbued the simple words with an odd intensity.

I hooked the last two pieces together to make a circle again.

"Look at this." Marcus commanded. He leaned over the table, holding out his phone.

With the bracelet in my hand, I reached for the device. I caught a glimpse of a picture on the screen. As I touched the corner of the phone, a high-pitched whine sounded. The picture scrambled.

Grimacing, I pulled away, bracelet and all. The noise stopped and the picture returned.

Shocked, I glanced at Rabi. I stared at the pattern etched in the metal. I repeated the action with the same result. Realization dawned.

Marcus jabbed his finger at the bracelet. "That thing has an electric current built into it."

"A magnetic key." Rabi spoke as if that explained everything. "Special lock."

Kevin drummed his hands on the sofa. "This is the security measure Reilly put in place for whatever is in the briefcase that Mrs. Colchester learned about. The one the police have in their possession."

"You going to keep it?" My son pointed to the bracelet.

"I'm going to hide it." I flipped it over my shoulder, looking only in time to see Kevin catch it in mid-air. Before I could blink he tossed it to Rabi.

The other man slid it into his inner jacket pocket and zipped the pocket closed without comment.

Relief filled me and I scooted on to the sofa. My shoulders slumped against the cushion. "At least I solved the mystery of the cat. Now for what's in the briefcase. Could someone bypass the lock? Cut through the hinges, maybe?"

"Booby traps." Rabi's tone added a weight of certainty to his words. "Acid. Directed charges. Fire."

"Haigh has experience with explosives. Reilly couldn't have done all this by himself." Of course, few would question if a wealthy man demanded security measures.

Marcus rubbed his hands together. "No cheating. They need the key."

"To what?" A briefcase is only so big. What could it hold? "What's the most bang for your buck if you're moving oodles of money?"

We all eyed Kevin, who was the only one among us who'd ever dealt with any amount of wealth.

"For a businessman like Reilly it's got to be bearer bonds," Kevin said. "No question."

Marcus cocked his head to one side. "Like in *Die Hard*? The papers that blew up in the end and fell on the street?"

"Exactly." Kevin, fresh from a day of installing drywall, spoke casually of pricy bonds raining down from the sky. "They're not sold in the US any longer. Eurobonds are still issued. Developing countries sell them."

"Bearer bonds." Our son slowly repeated the words. "Like, if you have them, you get the money? Blank checks?"

My hubby smiled at the boy's incredulous tone. "When they were more common, they led to a lot of crime and theft. My uncle once walked out of a hotel with a two-inch stack of paper that was worth millions of dollars."

"It's an interesting theory." My mind raced through the possibilities. I didn't want to get ahead of myself. "There's no proof."

Kevin snapped his fingers in a rapid beat. It was a sure sign he was thinking through a problem. "Why would Reilly tie up his money in bearer bonds? If he was planning to bolt, he could have a bank account in the Caribbean. Those bonds are dangerous."

"Jewels?" Marcus added extra warmth to the word. His eyes sparkled. He looked like the pirate from his video game. "Diamonds? They'd fit in a briefcase."

"Harder to cash in." The furrows on Kevin's forehead only deepened. "Same argument. Why tie up any amount of money when you can hide it in an off-shore account? Electronic transfers can move and hide funds in the blink of an eye."

"If he was going on the run, he couldn't afford to lose money." I dissected the problem for possible answers. "Forensic accountants can track hidden accounts. I don't need more questions. I have very few answers as it is."

"Calm down, Belden." He waved away my agitation with a cavalier attitude. "If the detecting biz was easy, anyone could do it. You Beldens are the best."

Marcus stroked Mr. Pickles, who'd sauntered back and draped himself across the boy's lap. "Yeah, we got this."

I rolled my eyes at the pair of them.

Kevin rubbed my shoulder. Pulling me close, he kissed my cheek, laughing as he did so. "It's bearer bonds. The why is your problem."

"Thanks, sweetie." His teasing loosened the knots in my brain. I'd been beating myself up for nothing. I'd only been on the case for two days. The police were investigating as well. The answers would come in time.

For now, I turned to the practical side of the problem. "Where would the money have come from? Beverly swears their company is clean. The books have been audited for several years. She promised she'd turned him into the cops if anything was fishy and I believe her."

Kevin looked at me as a cunning grin spread across his face. "Is it stealing if the money came from his own company? He could have done dozens of jobs on the side and pocketed the money. No record. No fraud."

"What's wrong with me?" His explanation hit me like a bolt from the blue. "I told myself the same thing earlier. Lorelei got nervous because Reilly's been traveling and working even more than his usual workaholic hours. He must have done extra jobs or created designs without committing to overseeing the building. He was famous for his innovative designs."

Mrs. C clicked her tongue. "It comes back to the dead man's motives, not the killer's. Reilly needed money that wasn't on record so he could create a new life. Or several, best to have options, don't you know?"

I smiled to myself. She would know. The older woman had used multiple identities while on the run for fifty years.

Pulling my feet close to my body, I pressed the soles together, planted my elbows on my knees, and leaned forward to stretch my spine. "You're absolutely correct, Mrs. C. The clues point to Reilly as an embezzler. Lester may have confronted him at the time, told him to come clean. Reilly killed him and dumped his body in the foundation."

Kevin stroked my arm, sending a warmth through my veins. "Life was good until the new plaza was planned for the same location. Reilly fought against it, but it was only a matter of time until he lost."

I carry on with the scenario. "He does jobs off the books. Consultations for direct fees. He stashes it all against the day he has to leave his life behind."

"His company." Rabi observed quietly. "His money."

"Good point, lad." Mrs. C pierced Rabi with a sharp stare. "He could have siphoned off a boodle of money from his own accounts and none the wiser before his oldest came home. You can't steal from yourself can you?"

"Follow the money!" Marcus threw up both arms as he yelled. "That's always a good motive. Who knew he had the goods?"

"Paul Findlay is an obvious choice." Kevin pointed to Rabi, who had the bracelet and its hidden clue. "No way Reilly moved that much money without his accountant knowing. They've been together for decades. Smart money says Findlay knew the bracelet was the key."

I scanned the board. "If he knew, did his wife know? She certainly was interested in the collar. I wonder what time Brooke Findlay's Las Vegas dinner ended. Reilly could have died any time from midnight to six in the morning."

Mrs. C pointed a dangerous looking knitting needle at me. "Three hours up and back from Vegas. She could have done him in, couldn't she?"

My narrowed gaze settled on the whiteboard's timeline. "That collar wasn't on Rookie when I was at the house with Lorelei on Saturday. Someone put it on the cat between then and Monday morning. Why put it on a cat?"

"Reilly wouldn't do that." Kevin's eyes narrowed. "He needed the bracelet with him, if he had to take off suddenly. Unless... Findlay kept it as a security measure."

Rabi watched the exchange silently. He'd said many times that he liked to listen to the plots and theories unfold. The call to action was his specialty.

Marcus started gyrating and snapping his fingers around his head. "That's why the case is booby trapped. Reilly and Findlay didn't trust each other. I bet they each kept one thing with them."

Rabi gave the boy a thumbs up.

Mrs. C's knitting needles clicked away. Her wrinkles around her eyes had multiplied as she concentrated. "Could be Lorelei found it? Nay, there's no bottom to that basket, is there?"

Marcus popped up and grabbed an orange marker. "Rookie didn't go far. She was in the bushes the whole time."

I gasped suddenly as a possibility hit me. "What if Findlay is the bomb-maker? If Reilly was leaving, that might explain why he destroyed part of his house."

Kevin's skepticism was written all over his face. "Why would he plant a bomb in his house?"

"Cover his tracks." My brain whirled like a kaleidoscope on steroids. I gasped as a bolt from my brain shot through me. "Reilly planned to disappear. With him missing and his beloved mansion partially destroyed, the police would think Reilly was dead. Tiffany said her brother would never blow up that building. He loved it. Besides, he blamed Haigh for getting the Drake demolished. When Reilly skipped town, Haigh would be a suspect. He could throw the blame on the gallery owner as a final act of revenge."

The wild theory didn't interrupt Mrs. C's knitting for a second. But she did eye me with a skeptical look. "Mr. Reilly blew up his house to buy himself more time?"

Give me a break. It was all I had.

Marcus bounced a squeaky mouse toy above Mr. Pickles outstretched paws. "The place was only partially damaged. He couldn't bring himself to flatten the whole house."

"It's a possibility." It was the only theory so far that explained Reilly planting the bomb. I chewed my lip as I considered the angles. When a crossword puzzle is complete the answers flow together. So far this case was not flowing. "I'm not convinced it's the right answer."

"What if the Findlays stole the bonds then blew up the house to cover their tracks?" Marcus's eyes sparkled at his new theory. He struggled to get the toy away from Mr. Pickles as one long claw caught the mouse. "Reilly found out. He and Findlay argued and Reilly was killed."

Rabi tapped the boy's arm. "Reilly planted the bomb."

"Dadgummit." The boy frowned over the swearword from my Kentucky childhood. "A flaw in my plan."

The cat flipped onto his stomach, still holding the captured stuffed mouse. He thrust his head forward as if listening. His piercing green eyes lit on me like a laser.

Was he trying to tell me something? If so, I wasn't receiving the message. I also didn't need the added pressure from a cat.

Marcus tapped his chin. "Reilly was planning to run off the day he was killed. No one knew he was in town until Lorelei saw him."

Kevin grunted. "She wasn't supposed to be home."

"Exactly." Marcus pointed at Kevin. "But Haigh was staking out his house. He's been stalking Reilly for years. Haigh saw him return and saw your client hit her husband."

"Suddenly she's *my* client?"

Marcus didn't miss a beat. "Haigh tried to stop Reilly. They argued, and there's a dead guy. Plus, Haigh takes the bonds. Millions of dollars. He's in the South of France."

Mrs. C nodded approval. "That hits all the corners to a picture, it does."

I couldn't follow her British slang, but that didn't stop me jumping on the wagon with the older woman. "I like it. If only the evidence would back it up."

Kevin raised a brow, obviously skeptical. "There are plenty of theories that could fit the few facts we know."

So true. I refused to abandon this one. "Haigh taking the bonds adds an interesting angle, except we decided they're in the briefcase at the police station."

Mrs. C once again stabbed a knitting needle in my direction, coming dangerously close to my feet. "How much money could he have collected, do you think? Two years he's been padding his secret account?"

"Five." Rabi interjected. "New plaza proposal. Five years."

Kevin's gaze strayed to the boards. "Reilly knew as soon as that building came down, he had to be ready to run."

Mrs. C and Marcus exchanged an excited look. "We could check on his rates and projects. Come up with a rough figure perhaps, eh? I can make a few calls tomorrow."

Marcus eyed me with a hopeful gleam in his eyes. "What could it hurt?"

Anything. Everything.

The hopeful note in their voices fed my desperation to find something solid. With those two rogues, complications could easily multiply. I wasn't certain an estimate on the amount of the bonds would help, but it couldn't hurt. I also had few other options.

Mrs. C could spin chaos out of string. Nonetheless, I gave her the nod. "Go ahead. See what you can find."

She grabbed the yarn and flung out her arm, pulling thread loose. "That's the ticket."

Kevin's fingers tapped a silent message on my shoulder. His expression was thoughtful. "How would Haigh have known about the bonds? The accountant and his wife, I understand. If Reilly was leaving on Monday, who caught on to the last game of Reilly's life?"

Brooke? If the accountant's wife knew about the money, would she kill to get it?

I had to find out about the dinner she attended. If she retired early, she wasn't accounted for. Of course, neither was Haigh. So far.

Paul Findlay? The man who'd known Reilly for decades. If anyone knew Reilly had the bonds, Findlay did. How much money would it take to drive someone to kill?

Too bad Paul Findlay's alibi was rock solid. The police had the security tape of the convenience store.

I'd failed to see the tape earlier, but tomorrow I intended to visit Wilson and watch the tape that cleared Paul Findlay of murder.

And rid me of my best suspect.

13

— • —

41 Across; 8 Letters

Clue: An intense longing

Answer: Yearning

Wednesday morning, I woke up nice and warm, snuggled against Kevin. I was in that delicious limbo between sleeping and waking. Did I have time to lay in bed for five more minutes? Or should I get up and start the day?

That's when the ringing phone punched me in the gut.

"Not three mornings in a row." Feeling Kevin stiffen saved me from having to keep silent. I gritted my teeth. "I'm going to throttle someone."

I grabbed the phone and swiped the screen before I realized… "It's not me."

Kevin groaned and sat up. "Hello?"

I hugged his warm pillow to my chest and smiled in relief. This morning I was the one listening to a one-sided conversation.

"Any damage?" Pause. "They shut off the water?"

Someone's house flooded. Hopefully it wasn't our fault. No way, my brain shot back. Kevin was too careful.

"Yeah, I'll be right out." Another pause. "Why did they call you? Oh, yeah."

I hugged the pillow tighter. "Jimbo? The drywall job?"

"Yeah." Kevin rubbed his face and stretched his arms above his head. "The father-in-law was playing plumber and hit a pipe. Jimbo texted them last night and they hit re-dial."

"It's on you this time. Ha-ha." And then my phone rang. I clutched the pillow and buried my head in its softness. "No! No! No!"

"Ha-ha! It's you." Kevin barely got the words out before he burst out laughing on his way to the bathroom.

I swiped my thumb across my phone. I glanced at the screen as I brought it to my ear. Talk about déjà vu. "Yes, Lorelei?"

Didn't the woman ever sleep in? She was rich. I was beginning to hope I could prove she *was* guilty of murder. Perhaps that would get her off my back. I let my hand holding the phone drift to one side until it was laying on my pillow.

"They arrested me!"

I winced at her shrill tone. Good thing the cell phone wasn't plastered by my ear.

"For murder!" She continued, still raising her voice.

I kept my eyes closed. I couldn't get too excited about this turn of events. "Well, that was kind of a given. What else would they charge you with? Jaywalking?"

This time I prepared for her scream by moving the phone farther away. I opened my eyes to the welcome sight of Kevin tucking in his work shirt while he smiled at me. I pointed at the phone. "Lorelei."

He nodded knowingly. "I heard."

A sharp knock sounded on the door. Guess who?

"Come in." Kevin had to raise his voice to be heard over Lorelei's steady stream of outrage.

The boy child frowned at me. "I'm a little kid. I need my sleep."

Mr. Pickles strolled past him and leapt onto the bed. He circled while he kneaded the comforter into a perfect pile for his nap.

My jaw dropped open. "I don't get to eat in this bed. How is he allowed to be up here?"

"Give him a break." Marcus rolled his eyes and pulled the cat into his arms. He slung the beast over his shoulder. "He's new to the family."

When I blinked the sleep out of my eyes, Mr. Pickles had looped his body around Marcus's neck. His paws were draped over the boy's shoulders.

I narrowed my gaze to keep them in focus. It was like looking at a two-headed monster. Two eyes filled with innocence and two eyes with a dose of feline disdain stared into mine. "Mr. Pickles, you have a weird brother."

Marcus looked at me with a confused expression "What?"

"You were supposed to prevent this." My client's high-pitched words filled the moment of silence.

I grabbed my phone and reared to a sitting position, glaring at the readout. "I never promised you wouldn't be arrested for murder."

"You're supposed to be finding the real killer." Her voice rose an entire octave.

I didn't think that was possible.

Lorelei continued without pausing for breath. "If you'd done your job, I wouldn't be here. Have you done anything in the last three days? Were you sleeping just now?"

Her accusatory tone was like gasoline on an open flame. My temper flared to a hot nine. "Of course, I was sleeping! It's six-thirty in the morning! And your husband died two days ago, not three. It was Monday. This is Wednesday. During that time, I've interviewed everyone involved in this case."

Except for Haigh and Brooke Findlay.

And I adopted two cats.

I left both of those statements out.

"Oh, dear." The British accent left no question as to the speaker's identity. "Bit of a to do, eh?"

"Do you know who's guilty?" Desperation mixed with hope in Lorelei's voice.

The evidence points to you. However, my gut and my puzzle don't agree.

"I have a few ideas." Nothing definite since I hadn't eliminated anyone and I couldn't prove anything. As we both took a breath some of the woman's shrill rantings filtered through my brain. Especially, the "get down here and get me out" part. "Lorelei, are you at the station?"

"Yes."

I had a bad feeling about where this was headed. "Was I your one call?"

"Of course." She went into high octave. She sounded surprised that I had to ask. "Who else would I call?"

That wasn't obvious? "Your lawyer."

"Tracy, you are the only person on this planet who believes I'm innocent." She exhaled heavily. "And you don't even like me."

She was right. On both counts. And I didn't feel one bit guilty. I don't have to like everyone. "The police must have something new on you if they arrested you."

No answer. I ran a hand through my short hair. Let me think. What would this woman do? A bored, rich, entitled... Had she mentioned a designer on the east coast? "Were you leaving town by chance? After they told you not to?"

"I don't see the harm in a weekend shopping spree in New York City." She spoke in an aggrieved tone. "I planned to return."

"Of course, you did. Except that city has an international airport." I made a face at the phone. "The police told you not to leave Langsdale."

"That Wilson person is rude and self-righteous," she said, not answering my question. "You need to get over here. Now. The cops have to share evidence with the defense."

I scanned my in-house audience and gestured to the phone, looking for sympathy. "Lorelei, that's for lawyers at the trial. I can't do anything."

"Oh, please. You're the pushiest broad I know," she paused for breath, or possibly for effect. "And that's including me."

Grandad always said go with your strength.

Nods were exchanged among the peanut gallery. Mr. Pickles, still draped on Marcus like a cape, seemed to nod in unison with the boy child. Couple that with the cat's unblinking stare and it looked like the cat was judging me.

Being put on trial by a feline was very disturbing to my pre-coffee brain.

"That may be true." I spoke to Lorelei regarding the pushy comment. "But Wilson doesn't have to tell me anything. He knows I'm not a lawyer."

"Talk to him," Lorelei pleaded. "I'm innocent and you're the only one who believes me. I'm your client. You have to save me."

How had I gotten myself into this fix? I actually didn't trust Lorelei as far as I could throw her BMW. I'd simply weighed the evidence. She had the means and the opportunity, but her plan to blackmail her living husband would have put her in the driver's seat regarding the divorce. She believed she'd lose a fortune with her husband's death.

Confronted and taunted with her own infidelity would she have attacked him? Possibly. She was still on my list as a suspect. But beneath her entitled fluff, Lorelei was too cold-blooded to strike out in anger.

In her own way, she was as much of a game-player as any con artist. She simply played for different stakes. The Feilens rarely lost, but when they did, they knew another mark was as close as tomorrow. Lorelei could have landed a rich old fool within three weeks of her divorce.

I threw up my hands. Arguing was getting me nowhere. "I'll be down after I get dressed."

Lorelei disconnected without saying goodbye.

"That's it then." Mrs. C turned on her pink slippers. "I'll get the pancakes and bacon on. Soon as Rabi stops in, we'll get him up to speed. He'll be happy to pop you round to school while your mum and dad toddle off, eh?"

"I'll set the table." With the cat draped over his shoulders, Marcus followed the older woman. Then he and Mr. Pickles glanced at me. "Text me with any juicy updates and don't solve the murder until after school."

I threw my phone on my end-table. "Of course, I'll schedule all the confessions around your classroom hours."

***

After a leisurely breakfast and an update with the gang, I toddled down to the station and spoke with Detective Wilson. At the moment, I was sitting in his office drinking coffee. Pretty decent I had to admit.

Despite what Lorelei chose to believe, the police did not believe I'd become a lawyer overnight. Therefore, they weren't obligated to update me on their investigation. A fact Wilson took great pleasure in telling me.

At which point I took even more pleasure in informing him of my progress with the other suspects. Some details he knew: knowledge of Brandon Haigh's argument with Reilly and the addendum to the will giving Lorelei a settlement and even more motive for murder. I updated him on the bearer bonds theory.

I did not discuss the bracelet. Always keep an ace up your sleeve.

Between my leisurely breakfast, him keeping me waiting, and a bit of back and forth, it was now late morning. I was alone as he'd been called away to follow up on an incoming report.

I inhaled the strong roast coffee as I sorted through the clues in my puzzle. The entire bottom half refused to come together.

The door opened with a creak and slammed shut with a clatter.

"What are you thinking, Tracy?" Wilson's mocking tone was full of bravado. He had a long, lanky build. He reminded me of a scarecrow who'd jumped off his pole and walked out of the cornfield. His thin, blond hair added to the impression.

I took a sip of coffee, eyeing him over the rim. "I'm wondering if you actually charged Lorelei with murder. Do you have additional evidence? Or is it possible you didn't want her fleeing? In which case you might be holding her on a forty-eight-hour warrant?"

Wilson pointed at me with his left hand and pulled the imaginary trigger. "We got nothing new. Technically, she's in as a material witness. We have time until something else turns up. The DA won't let her go."

I waved the thought away. "I didn't expect them to."

"Then why are you taking up room in my office?"

I fished around in the dark pool of my mind. A couple of things stood out. "Two items. First, were Kevin and I the only people who were asleep at two o'clock on Monday morning?"

Wilson exhaled a weary sounding sigh. "Tell me about it. Midnight to six a.m. and half of the suspects were wandering the streets. Only three of them were allegedly in bed. I'd love to arrest them all. What's the second thing?"

I took a drink of coffee. The dark brew warmed my throat and fired my synapses. "Any updates on the time of death? The M.E. can't narrow it down from six hours? What about the liver temperature test they talk about on TV? What about the autopsy?"

The man rewarded me with a frown. "I love being compared to the well-groomed detectives who have designer squad rooms and get lab results in ten minutes."

"It's a burden we all bear." I liked Wilson. He was a good guy. He usually listened to my input, which, of course, made him a genius. "Come on, fill me in."

He ran his fingers through his limp cornstalk-colored hair. "The enzyme test got screwed up. Interference from some drug Reilly was taking. They had to re-run the lab work. The cold, wet weather and the victim being in shirtsleeves played havoc with the time of death."

"It's been over forty-eight hours." Wilson was holding something back. "You have to have an update."

The detective's mouth curled. "You're so stubborn."

I smacked his desk with the flat of my hand. "Gimme."

"The M.E. shortened the window. Reilly was dead by three-thirty at the latest, maybe three. He was alive as late as twelve-thirty."

I bit my lip. "He might have been murdered when Kevin and I were in the street after the bomb exploded?"

Wilson nodded. "Or your client killed him before calling you."

"That reminds me. Was there an injury to the back of his head where Lorelei admits to hitting him?"

His brow furrowed in thought. "Nothing on the autopsy. She didn't hit him hard enough to leave a mark."

"That doesn't make sense." The clues had to be accounted for. A crossword puzzle wasn't finished until all the squares were filled in. "She whacked him with a bat. He was unconscious."

"And now he's dead." Wilson spoke slowly. "See how that works? He recovered. She followed him. The repeated blows destroyed evidence of the first. The time still works to incriminate her."

The M.E.'s update did me no good. "The new times don't clear anyone."

"Except Paul Findlay."

A frisson of excitement shot through my veins. "Brooke Findlay went to bed early Sunday night, didn't she? Tell me. I'll find out anyway."

The man shot me a sideways glance. "Brooke Findlay was last seen at eight-thirty on Sunday night."

"Three hours from Vegas. Confront Reilly. Kill him."

"In the middle of a grassy path?"

"There's a parking lot twenty yards from where Reilly was found. There wouldn't have been any witnesses at that time of night. Then, she drives back in time for breakfast."

"Are you done?"

"I want to see the security tape of Paul Findlay at the convenience store."

Wilson met my gaze. The grimace on his face looked more disgusted than stubborn. "I can't."

"You owe me, Wilson." I honestly thought the guy would cooperate. Several months ago, I handed him a case that solved four murders. "Be a good kindergartener. You share. I'll share. If not, I'm going to lose your phone number."

He threw himself against his chair. His expression grew darker. "The server it was stored on is down. The computer geeks think the server got exposed to malware. The IT department is working on it."

His excuse was too intricate to be fake. Disgusted, I raked my hands through my hair. I wasn't sure how much good my seeing the tape would do. Wilson was a good cop. However, I still pounded my fists on his desk in frustration. "Any estimate on time to recovery?"

"Yeah," Wilson answered in an eager tone. His eyes lit up. "An hour ago. Twenty minutes ago. Ten minutes from now. Next week. Take your pick."

My glare did nothing to diminish his self-satisfied smile. "How could you not make a copy? You're going to need that tape for trial."

"No, I don't." Wilson scoffed. He thrust his shoulders forward. "The tape clears Findlay. The forensic team made a compilation of the camera footage that tracked the guy's trip through town. I watched it with them. We were finishing a second review when the computer team took the server down. They didn't have time to copy the tape."

Just my luck, the computers were against me. "The companies still have their records. Did you contact them for more copies? Make another compilation."

Wilson swept to his feet. "Absolutely, your majesty. We live to serve. We have nothing else to do. There's no other crime in Langsdale, except for a brawl at an auction that sent two guys to the hospital. I spent an afternoon at the hospital and arrested them both for assault. Then the DA made a plea deal and they're out."

"Good." I refused to be put off by his sarcasm. "When can I see the new tape?"

"You're beyond annoying, Tracy." He plopped in his chair. "Watch my lips. The tape clears Findlay. I saw it. Street cameras. A few business cameras. The convenience store. The camera and alarm on the Findlay residence. He left a clear trail through town."

"How convenient for him." See? I can do sarcasm, too. The whole episode also sounded too convenient.

The detective ignored me. "He signed out of his office building at eleven-twenty-two p.m. He stopped for gas. He was in the convenience store from eleven-forty-eight until twelve-twenty. He drove home. He turned off the alarm, walked in, and reset the alarm. Nothing further until Monday morning when he left for work."

I growled at my rapidly cooling coffee. Not seeing the tape rankled, but I had to move on. Haigh was my next, best option. "I'll let it go, on one condition."

He gave me a fixed stare as he tapped a pencil on the desk. "This should be good."

"What did you find out about Haigh?" If Wilson could pin it on Haigh, could I really walk away? My stomach started flipping. I swallowed hard and put on a brave face. "Tell me the galleria man took a plane to the South of France late Monday after he killed Reilly. Extradite him for an arrest. Let's close this case and get Lorelei out of my life."

"I wish."

Relief washed over me. My bones felt weak. My gut loosened the knots. "What did you find out?"

Wilson studied me with an intense gaze. "I thought you wanted him to be guilty."

I gave a half-hearted shrug, trying to pull off an uncaring attitude. This is the problem when working with detectives. They're trained to detect.

"Why should I tell you anything?" Before I could blink, Wilson reared forward. His long thin hand hit his desk with resounding force. "I have you to thank for sending me to that warehouse full of paintings and statues. I was stuck there until eight o'clock last night. I didn't need another suspect courtesy of the Belden Gang."

"Hah!" I stabbed my finger at him. "You deserved it after pointing Amy Reilly in my direction for a lost cat."

"I was advancing your case." A flush crept up his neck and reached his cheeks.

"And I'm helping you solve another murder." I shouted, embracing the heated exchange with both hands. "Was Haigh even on your list until Wayne Scovell called?"

"You have no business being involved in a homicide investigation."

"It's my job." I pounded my chest. "Someone has to lay out the breadcrumbs for you. Tell me what you found."

He threw his hands in the air. "You're a P.I. not a cop."

"Fine, I'll leave." I ended on a loud yell. Then I took a breath and held up two fingers. "But first, tell me two things."

That's when he buried his head in his hands. "Not this again."

"Buck up, Wilson." I put my hand on the man's shoulder. "I'll buy you a lemonade when this is over."

He straightened and painted a surprised look on his face. "A lemonade? Be still my heart."

"You still owe me for those murders I helped you clear." My brain fired up to full alert. The Reilly case was open and I was on the hunt. "If you want me out of your office, tell me where Haigh went. Plane? Train? Automobile to Vegas? Do you have any idea regarding Haigh's movements this past weekend? Where is he? Dead or alive?"

For an answer, Wilson pulled a file out of his in-box and threw it open. "No trace of the man. No tickets out of Langsdale or Las Vegas. His car is accounted for. He has no relatives. No action on his credit cards since Sunday."

"That doesn't track." My gaze wandered over the desk and around the office. My brain searched for a clue. "Why hide now? He wanted to unmask Reilly's perceived crime of killing his brother."

The detective's expression took on a self-satisfied smirk. "If Reilly had this hidden stash on him, Haigh could have taken the money and run."

"You have the briefcase. Haigh had no hidden money." I chewed on my thumbnail. Where could the man be? How could a person hide in plain sight with no money and no credit? It wasn't like there was another body in this case.

Out of nowhere the picture Marcus had shown me of the victim caught and injured in the blast popped into my mind. I blinked in surprise. Why did that spring to mind?

My son's voice repeated in my memory how the guy looked like a mummy. The face had been swaddled in bandages from the injuries. I caught my breath as clues and answers aligned to an unexpected pattern. Could it be?

I grabbed Wilson's arm. "Have you identified the victim caught in the blast?"

Wilson tapped the papers in the file. If he was surprised by the change of topic, it didn't show. "Ivan Sullivan, two doors down. He works nights and was known for taking walks on the trail at odd hours. We figure he walked too close to the Reilly house at the wrong time."

I followed my own trail down a couple of rabbit holes before the squares in my puzzle were filled. "Sullivan is single, isn't he? Lives alone. Quiet. Rarely talks to his neighbors."

"You make him sound like a serial killer." Frustration sounded in Wilson's voice. His hands clenched into fists. "Other than that, you scored on all counts, but Sullivan didn't murder Reilly."

"He's not in the hospital either." It all came together in a blinding flash. "Sullivan is on vacation. Brandon Haigh's been stalking Reilly. He was injured in the explosion of the Reilly house. Haigh is your coma victim."

Wilson started to shake his head. Then, he stopped. The wheels in his head started turning. His long fingers jumped to the keyboard and he started typing.

I poked him in the shoulder. "Check Sullivan's credit cards."

The detective smacked my hand away. "Don't tell me how to do my job."

His short, angry tone told me he agreed with my latest guess. He was already checking activity on the neighbor.

Wilson grabbed his mouse and flipped through the report on the screen. A tense silence filled the office until, without warning, the man threw the mouse a short distance across his desk.

I waited for six, maybe seven endless seconds. "Come on. Tell me."

His expression settled into hard lines. "Breckenridge, Colorado for the past five days."

"Yes! Marcus had it pegged." I had to give credit where credit was due. "He said Haigh would be staking out Reilly's house. He knew Reilly was ready to disappear for good."

The detective grunted as he rubbed his chin. "He must have confronted Reilly when he recovered from Lorelei's blow. They might have fought."

"Might have?" The words exploded out of my mouth before I had time to think. "Haigh killing Reilly is more likely than Lorelei."

Wilson waffled his hand. "There's no proof either way and if it is Haigh in the hospital –"

"It is!"

"He's not going anywhere. One of them is the killer. Ta-da!"

When the man fell silent, I stabbed the file. Did he think he was done? I pulled myself up and faced him directly. "No, ta-da. There's still the matter of my client."

"Oh, that." Wilson responded in a flippant tone as if Lorelei's fate didn't matter. Then he sobered and shook his head. "You're not going to win this fight, Tracy. She was warned, and she's the best suspect."

"Lorelei Reilly is a self-centered, annoying woman." I had no illusions about her and no reason to defend her. "She's also a wealthy woman, a grieving widow, and, trust me, she'll be very convincing when she cries her crocodile tears in front of the cameras."

A cynical awareness hardened Wilson's expression. "So now she's your buddy."

"I'm tired of getting woken up by phone calls before the sun is up." I smacked his desk with my fist so hard his pencils jumped in time to the blows. "My husband's not thrilled about it either. And I'm more than willing to share the fun by making sure Lorelei has the private cell phone numbers of you, the DA, and the mayor. Don't think I won't."

I was digging myself a hole with the hardcore threat. Whether Lorelei deserved my loyalty or not, she was my client. I'd promised to fight for her.

Wilson refused to be goaded by my threats. He folded his hands over his stomach. "What do you suggest?"

Find the killer so I don't have to. The words were on the tip of my tongue, but I'd pushed Wilson far enough. He had the mayor, the media, and his captain demanding results. "If Lorelei stays in town, will the DA release her?"

"Why should he?"

"Because I need a carrot to wave in front of her nose." I fisted my hands in frustration. "That woman may have the answers to this murder."

His gaze grew distant as he considered my demand.

I pushed while I had an opening. "Put a tracker on her ankle. Put one on her car. Tell her if she tries to leave town again you'll lock her up for good. I'll warn her that one more stunt and I'll quit the case, 'cuz I'm ready to do it."

"Oh, we wouldn't want that, would we?"

I smiled at his sarcasm. "Lorelei is convinced the media and the police are going to railroad her for this murder. She's not too far off the mark."

Lorelei had reason to fear. She was a rich woman with three husbands behind her. Two were now dead. If she were put on trial, I'd bet money on her getting convicted.

A wistful looked lightened Wilson's tired face. "She's a perfect suspect. She was on site. She admits attacking him. He could have confronted her about her infidelity. She had the additional settlement at his death. She blew up and killed him. No one would have sympathy for her."

Except Wilson was too good a detective to railroad a suspect unless he believed in their guilt. "Lorelei knows I'll turn her in if she's guilty. She wouldn't be pushing me to find the killer if she murdered her husband."

I paused to let the words sink into the scarecrow's brain. "Let me talk to her, then tag her and let her loose. She won't cross me. She believes I'm her only hope."

"Poor woman." Wilson's sympathetic comment morphed into an evil smile. After a moment, he shrugged. "I'll sell it to the DA, without the cell phone threat. What's your next move?"

Good question. "There's no proof against anyone. I'll try to break the alibis of the family and friends. Tiffany Sweet lives only a couple of blocks away from where the body was found."

"Reilly was headed to her house when he was attacked." Wilson inserted. "She didn't receive or make any calls. She swears she was asleep."

"Like any normal person."

"Her neighbors didn't hear or see anything and two of them were awake. No visitors were seen coming or going. No barking dogs."

"She also has no motive." My only option was to keep poking at the other suspects. "The Newcombs could be covering for each other. Amy had time to sneak away from her friends."

The detective frowned. "Jeremy Newcomb's tall. He'd have the reach on Reilly. He's too quiet. I don't trust him. Pounding the head in? That's personal. The killer is someone Reilly personally wronged. Lorelei and Haigh are both good on that count."

I had to find out who. "I'll talk to my client. See if I can find out if she knew what the dead man was playing at."

***

Interview rooms in police stations all look the same. A wooden table, two or three chairs, and a mirror on one wall with a mic so the police can eavesdrop. Always remember that part, no matter what the police say.

Lorelei fluffed her blond curls as if the media were waiting outside the door, which they might be. "I knew you'd get me out."

I gestured to the drab walls. "You're not out."

Her lip quivered. "You're working on it, right? You and your buddy?"

"Detective Wilson isn't my buddy." Okay, he was kind of. How to bring this woman out of her own private dimension and back to reality? "He's speaking with the DA about releasing you, on the condition that you make no attempt to leave the city for any reason."

She nodded like a bobble-head doll.

Too quick. I stared at her without blinking. "If you leave Langsdale, I'll quit this case. I'll also make sure you spend time in prison if I have to make up a crime."

"You would. You're mean." Her hopeful expression melted into a quivering lip. "I don't like jail. It's scary and smelly, and so are those women."

A cell door slamming shut behind you had a way of sobering up anyone. "Give me ammunition for Wilson to give to the DA."

She eyes filled with tears. "I've told you and the police everything I know."

"Did your husband ever mention a man named Lester Jensen?"

Her jaw tightened. A mulish expression filled her gaze. She'd been questioned several times this week.

"Think, Lorelei." I softened my voice as my finger stabbed the scarred wooden surface of the tabletop. "I need another suspect. Reilly worked with Jensen right after college at the Dawson Firm."

Her violet eyes studied me intently. She bit her lower lip as she leaned forward, hanging on my words. When her face scrunched up, it looked like time for the waterworks. Then her golden eyes lit up like the springtime sun.

"The embezzlement guy." Her gaze grew distant. She tapped her chin. "Thaddeus spoke of him recently."

A jolt of hope shot through me. "When? Exactly."

"Five, six weeks ago at least." Her fingers tried to grip the table as the details returned. "It was odd because he'd never discussed the theft before. I don't know why he thought of it."

Because Haigh had done something. I prompted her further. "Did anything else happen that day?"

"Yes." Her voice rose as she jumped out of her chair. "We were leaving a restaurant with the Findlays when a man rushed at Thaddeus. He screamed that justice would be done. The Drake's demolition would see to it."

"What did the man look like?"

Furrows formed in her perfect brow. "Medium height. Brown, curly ponytail. Does that help?"

That was Haigh. I pressed my hands against the table. "What did your husband say about Lester Jensen, later?"

"Nothing much." She pressed her perfect pink lips together. "I asked him what the man meant about justice from the Drake. He said Lester Jensen had haunted the Drake since his crime and the end was near."

That was the closest thing to a confession anyone would ever hear from Reilly. Only a ghost could haunt a building.

"Wasn't Jensen the embezzler who ran off years ago?"

I nodded absently. It took me a moment to catch my breath. Haigh and Jensen had been tied together in Reilly's mind.

Lorelei grabbed my arm. "Is this connected with Thaddeus's murder? Did that man kill him? Go after him."

No need. As Wilson said, Haigh wasn't going anywhere. But I had to be sure. "Did your husband mention the cats lately?"

The other woman frowned as if I'd gone mad. "Never. The servants took care of them."

"Did he ever wear a bracelet? Metal? With lines on it?"

"Yes." She slapped the table. "He never wore jewelry until two years ago. He had that bracelet on his wrist every day since then. What was it for?"

"What did he say?"

"That it was a gift from Paul Findlay. A security measure." Lorelei's eyes gleamed. Her hands trembled. "Is that enough for a get out of jail free card?"

"You'll get out." I promised. I felt a twinge of guilt since I'd already secured the deal. On the other hand, I hoped the woman would take the police warning seriously.

She'd solidified the case against Haigh, but where did this information leave me? None of these facts cleared her or indicted the injured man.

Lorelei was still the best suspect and if there was no break in the case, she might end up in a jail cell again. For my own conscience, I had to either prove her guilty or find the killer.

As for my case, I still didn't have any hard facts. Did the past get Reilly killed or was it his money that someone wanted?

Who had known about the briefcase and the bracelet? If I could find out those answers, I might be able to finger his murderer.

14

2 Across; 8 Letters
Clue: Forward movement toward a destination or a goal
Answer: Progress

Within thirty minutes of Lorelei's hopeful question, Wilson came through with the free pass.

I repeated my threats.

Lorelei delivered promises of good behavior.

No telling how long that would last.

The legal process is thorough but it's not quick. When I stepped into the light of day, it was the middle of the afternoon.

I discovered my significant other was once again working hard. Left to my own devices, I set my sights on Brooke Findlay. The timeline made her a suspect, one I hadn't spoken with. Her husband's knowledge of the bearer bonds added to her possible guilt. I didn't have high hopes that she knew the details of Reilly's departure, but she might know more than me.

Several frustrating calls later I confirmed my target was out of town. Further updates didn't help my mood. The M.E. hadn't released Reilly's body which delayed the funeral, now planned for Thursday evening.

Turns out, Amy had gone to San Francisco to rehearse her part in a possible play.

As for Beverly Reilly and Jeremy Newcomb, guess where Lorelei got the idea to fly to New York? Yep, the happy pair flew to the east coast to re-open their loft apartment.

Wilson had kept a few aces in his sleeve. The rat. The Reilly daughters were due back tomorrow morning for their father's memorial service that evening.

Every other major suspect was free to leave town?

So much for Lorelei being a material witness. The DA was desperate. I'd give odds my client was forty-eight hours from being charged with murder.

All because I couldn't get inside the head of a deceitful dead man.

The Case of the Deceitful Dead Man. That sounds like the title of a Perry Mason book.

Don't tell Marcus I said that.

My next course of action was to call Wilson back. We yelled at each other some more. I hadn't expected him to take my call. At this point our interactions were like therapy for both of us, but cheaper.

The only path left to me was doing actual work. I went home and shifted to my B&T handyman profession. After a few hours of updating the financial spreadsheets, ordering supplies for upcoming jobs, and e-mailing clients, I was in a better mood.

Rabi had agreed to pick up Marcus from an after-school soccer match. They arrived within minutes of Kevin coming home. Mrs. C joined us.

The Haigh revelation garnered a big reaction.

I high fived Marcus who basked in deserved praise.

The rest of the update took all of five minutes and that included the question-and-answer period.

Lorelei was out of jail.

The other suspects were out of town. All due back tomorrow. No solid proof of anyone's guilt.

Kevin read my depressed mood and took charge at that point. He declared a jigsaw puzzle night and we made homemade pizza.

I put my brain and the case on hold. It was lovely.

***

Thursday morning when I woke up the clock read six-twenty-five. Neither of our phones had rung and the alarm hadn't gone off. I smiled in relief and rolled over to hug my husband.

When Marcus knocked on the door, Kevin kissed me again then eyed the door and raised a brow in question.

I shook my head. "I'm choosing not to hear anything. My mornings have been disturbed too often this week."

The knocking on our door changed to pounding. "I know you're in there. You have to answer me. I could be dying out here in the great cat uprising."

Kevin chuckled. "Come in."

The boy child swung open the door while two cats bolted past his legs and pounced on the bed. "Did I miss my early morning phone call? You didn't wake me."

"That's not funny." I glanced at the feline pair before meeting Marcus's gaze. "But I promise to set your alarm for two-thirty tomorrow morning if you'd prefer."

Rookie glided over the comforter straight toward me. She rubbed her head against my arms.

It would be rude not to pet her. I stroked her soft fur. That's when she leaned against me and started to purr. "Cat, you're such a schmoozer."

Mr. Pickles used the distraction to his own advantage. He stretched out on Kevin's side at the foot of the bed, well beyond my reach.

I swear he was laughing at me.

Kevin stroked the cat as he walked around the end of the bed. It had taken him only minutes to get dressed. "I'll start the coffee."

The ringing of my phone cut off any response. I screamed at the ceiling before burying my head in my hands. "If this is Lorelei, there might be another murder. You both have to alibi me."

"Steady on, Belden." Laughter underlined Kevin's voice. A tapping sounded to my right. "It's Wilson."

I raised my head to see my hubby tapping my cell phone on the end-table. A quick swipe of my thumb and I put Wilson on speaker. I warned him as such. "What do you know?"

"Good morning to you, too." Wilson's voice carried a note of triumph. "You owe me an entire pitcher of lemonade. The server's up. I have the Findlay tape if you still want to see it. Fifteen minutes."

This time a wave of caffeine carried me to the station in record time. I'd thrown on jeans and a top, filled up my mug, and headed for the door.

I figured once I viewed the tape, I could eliminate Findlay in my own mind. Then, I could dig on the other suspects or look for evidence against Haigh.

I had to make progress. Every tick of the clock counted against Lorelei. For the second morning in a row, I found myself sitting by Wilson's desk waiting for him to return. I'd barely arrived when he'd been called away. It was almost as if he had something in his life besides me.

For now, I was alone with his locked computer and a pile of folders. Not having any scruples, I flipped through the folders and pulled out Reilly's.

Within seconds, Wilson strode into the office like he owned the place. "Find what you wanted?"

"Not really," I admitted. "Your handwriting is atrocious. What's this about his finances? Are they clean?"

He pulled it out of my hands, eyeing me with a stern look. "Do you ever do your own work?"

"I try not to." I gave him a cheeky grin. Despite his words, he seemed in a good mood. "Is Reilly's money in order? Beverly said there was no funny business, but she's a suspect and I don't have a forensic accounting department."

The lanky looking scarecrow barely glanced at the folder before grabbing it out of my hands. He slipped it amongst the others. "Not a dollar out of place. Reilly's finances are squeaky clean."

I told him Kevin's theory about how Reilly earned money and kept it off the books.

"Kevin would know." Wilson signed onto his computer and tapped at the keyboard. "You think money is the motive for Reilly's murder?"

"Money or passion." One or both of those motives lay at the bottom of most murders. "Enough money will undermine any loyalty. Reilly had five years to earn and stash liquid funds. He could have had millions. He knew Haigh was closing in and the Drake was coming down."

The view on the computer screen changed.

"You got it?" Pulling my chair around the desk, I looked over Wilson's right shoulder.

As he brought up the footage, he glanced at me. "The only reason I'm doing this is because you don't have a gold shield and you've gotten lucky in the past."

I sneered at him. "Luck has nothing to do with my success."

The detective chuckled. "Yeah, stubbornness accounts for most of your record and the crazed Belden voice in your brain does the rest."

"Whatever works." My gaze was glued to the screen as the tape started to play.

The image showed Findlay on the street outside his office. He wore the tan hat with a wide brim along with the matching scarf Wanda had mentioned. He took the hat off and readjusted it before getting in his car. There was a distance shot of him getting gas. At last, the tape switched to him entering the convenience store. "You can't see his face with the hat and scarf."

"His wife bought the logo wear several weeks ago. His staff confirmed he's worn them every day since."

I followed Findlay's every move with an intentness that surprised even me. Something seemed odd. "Do you ever see his face?"

"The tape in his office building shows his face." Wilson assured me. "You saw him sign out. Street cameras picked up the car at several intervals until he went into the store."

I noted the facts, still staring at the screen. What was I looking for? Findlay was a big guy. His silhouette against the windows in his office flashed through my mind. He wasn't as bulky as Reilly but they were roughly the same height, same wide shoulders. Why was I thinking about Reilly?

Wilson put his hand next to my eye. He made a pinching motion with his finger and thumb.

"Is the little Belden voice talking to you yet?" he asked in a sing-song tone.

"Get away from me." I chuckled and slapped at his hand without looking. On the screen Findlay turned a corner to his left. The camera caught him full frame as his right foot kicked out and he swiveled on his left foot.

I froze as the air left my lungs.

The tape continued to play.

What had I just seen? "Rewind."

Wilson leaned forward. "What?"

I shoved the detective aside and grabbed the mouse. "That scene where he turned the corner."

The tape reversed, then ran forward. Again and again and again, I rewound those few seconds.

"Stop it!" Wilson grabbed the mouse away from me and froze the tape. "You're giving me a headache. What are you looking at?"

For a moment, I couldn't breathe. This is what happens when you ask the wrong questions, you get the wrong answers. I drew myself up in the chair and faced the man.

"I followed Reilly for a week before he died." I pointed to the frozen screen. "I have pictures and video of him. When he turns left, his right foot kicks out. I never figured out whether it was an affectation or an injury."

Wilson looked at me through a narrowed gaze. "He had a hip injury in college. Wore a brace for four months, supposed to have healed perfectly."

We stared at each other as the air thickened.

Without a word, I retook possession of the mouse. I ran the tape until I caught the figure in the profile. Then I stilled the image.

I replayed two scenes in my mind. Reilly at the poolside of a hotel on the northern hills outside of town with his secretary. Paul Findlay in his office. A beached whale next to an orca. Both big in their own way, but different. "Reilly has more meat on him. Findlay's got a beer belly."

Wilson looked from me to the screen and back. "Are you saying what I think you're saying?"

"That's Reilly." I was certain of it. I pointed at the screen, barely able to breathe. My mental crossword clues realigned. "I'd bet two gray cats on it."

The detective was on me like a short haired pointer on a pheasant. "You have two gray cats?"

I clamped my mouth shut two seconds too late. I should have realized that of everyone involved, Wilson would be the one who would keep track of the missing cats.

His narrowed gaze locked on me. "Twenty pounds plus? With six or more toes on their paws?"

"Oh, please. The animal shelter on the south side is overflowing with cats. Marcus got a matched pair of grays." I used my most scathing tone. It helped to hide the fact that while both statements were true, they didn't actually tie together. I never said Marcus got the cats from the shelter.

Wilson's stern expression didn't change. "If I go to your apartment, I'm not going to see the Reilly cats? I'll have to confiscate them."

Laughter burst out of my mouth. "Wilson, if you touch Marcus's new pets, between Kevin, Rabi, and that old British woman, they're not going to find enough of your body parts to bury. Besides, I told Lorelei. She's the owner and she's completely unconcerned."

The man snorted and sat back. "Then you better come clean, Tracy. Why is Amy Reilly frantic to find those cats?"

"Cat," I corrected. "Singular, the female was the only one she was after and it was Brooke who put her up to that stunt. Brooke, wife of Reilly's accountant, who knew about the briefcase with a fortune in bearer bonds."

He made a rolling motion with his hand. "Keep talking and I'll forget about stolen animals and withholding information."

"Save yourself. Marcus rescued strays." Which was sort of true. That's when I played my bracelet ace with the electrical wiring and the magnetic key for the briefcase. It took a bit of doing after his initial confusion. I followed that up with the booby traps. "My demolition expert—"

"We have one of those."

"I'm sure you do," I said, "mine told me the case could be set to release acid, a directed charge, or start a fire if it was opened without the key."

The light went on in his puzzled gaze. "Flipping the parts of that bracelet bypasses the booby traps and opens the lock?"

"In theory." I went for a know-it-all expression. "When the pieces are aligned, the random pattern changes to a copy of some electrical current thing. Ask Marcus. It gives off a charge that messed up Marcus's phone."

He fixed me with a hard stare. "Give."

I smiled at him. "Bearer bonds would make a nice retirement for a struggling police detective."

He pointed at me. "Or a P.I. who's working three jobs on the poor side of town."

We had a stare down for a few seconds.

I broke the stalemate with a laugh. "I'll have to bring you the bracelet."

As if on cue, both of us shifted our attention to the figure frozen on the screen.

"If that's Reilly…" The detective's long, skinny hand slammed on the desk. "Findlay planted the bomb. He was at the scene and he doesn't have an alibi for Reilly's murder."

The larger implications hit me like a plank of drywall. With another suspect on the scene, Lorelei might be in the clear.

"Let's not forget Findlay knew about the bonds. That's who Lorelei smacked with the bat." Which is why Reilly's body didn't have a bruise on the back of his head. The puzzle was finally coming together. "She made the same mistake we did. She saw a figure in the dark. When Reilly's body turned up, everyone assumed he'd been the man in the house."

"That was their plan," Wilson muttered. "Why?"

"Reilly didn't want to be seen in town?" I tried the idea on for size. "Did you find out what flight he was on?"

The lanky scarecrow detective shook his head. His frown deepened. "Nothing under his own name. We're checking the airport cameras to narrow down the specific flight he got off of, but so far we've got nothing.."

Swoosh! I love it when I score a hit. "Lorelei wasn't supposed to be home. Reilly wanted to avoid Haigh who he knew was stalking him. He sent Findlay to plant the bomb while he impersonated the accountant in case anything went wrong."

Wilson's gaze strayed to the image on the screen. "If Haigh accosted him, Findlay could reveal his identity and get rid of the man. They met after Findlay recovered, switched clothes-"

"Argued over the money. Reilly was killed and Findlay rushed home with his alibi intact." My voice rose in triumph as I rewrote the script for the night of the murder. "My client's in the clear. Pick up Findlay."

Wilson ran a hand through his lank hair and stared at me. "Better yet, tell me why Reilly arranged for Findlay to blow up his own house."

"Payback for Haigh. The man's been on Reilly's case for two years. He's argued with Reilly, threatened him. He was never going to quit. Reilly wanted to sow confusion in the wake of his disappearance. The police would look for Reilly's body, accost Haigh, the man who argued with him last month in public."

Wilson gave a half-nod. "If Reilly was dead, no one would look for him."

I sat back to get all my clues in order. "He pulled his daughters to town knowing he'd eventually have to leave. He wanted them to take over the company he built. But he couldn't risk anyone finding out he was hiding money. Beverly now had access to all the accounts."

"He had to get around her," Wilson interjected.

"Her and the law most likely." This was all supposition, but it laid a foundation for what happened. "This is where Paul Findlay, Reilly's long-time associate comes in."

Long lines deepened on Wilson's face. His jaw tightened.

I pointed at the screen. "That's Reilly. Findlay had experience with demolitions from his years of working on construction in college. He could have built the bomb and booby trapped the case."

"Why?" Wilson's yell echoed off the walls. "How? Brooke gave Findlay that hat and scarf weeks ago."

"Demolition of the Drake was first proposed five years ago. Reilly had time to plan every last detail." My gut and I agreed on this point. "Findlay convinced Brooke to order those souvenirs for the company. That would provide Paul the backstory for that night's game. Reilly has been planning for Monday morning for a long time."

"Thanks a lot." Wilson's bitter tone contrasted with his words. "Now I have to retrace every blank spot on the tape."

"Don't waste your time." I shot back. "They made the exchange off camera. Findlay planted the bomb at midnight and set a timer. He had to be at the house because he was the explosives expert. Reilly pretended to be Findlay, because Findlay needed an unimpeachable alibi. They believed the house was empty. But Lorelei was home and hit Findlay. He staggered to the pool and collapsed."

Wilson frowned and shook his head. "Findlay was wearing Reilly's coat. They switched cars and clothes."

"Lorelei said the man she hit wore the hood up on his mackintosh the entire time. She struck him from behind." After chasing him in a semi-drunken fury. A detail I skipped over. "He fell face down. This is why Reilly doesn't have a mark on the back of his head. Lorelei hit Findlay."

"Neither she nor Findlay turned the lights on, inside or outside the house." Wilson spoke in a thoughtful tone. "She never saw his face."

"She was hysterical." Even when she called me over an hour later. "I'm sure she barely touched his wrist to check for a pulse. I can't find my own pulse a lot of times."

Wilson shot me a stunned look. He started to speak, then switched tracks. "Findlay recovered, stumbled to the car, and drove off. He and Reilly met per their plan. Why did Reilly return to Langsdale? He should have had the case and the bracelet."

I had no answer for that question. My crossword puzzle had been completely rearranged after seeing the tape. "Something must have gone wrong. The bracelet ended up on Rookie. Maybe Findlay betrayed him. No, that doesn't make sense."

"The Findlay security camera shows him arriving home. He didn't leave all night long. Computer forensics shows no tampering with the security tapes."

I stared at the incriminating video. "Did it show his face? If Reilly installed the security program, he could have left a door off the grid. That way the record wouldn't show he'd left again."

Yes, I was making this up as I went along. That doesn't make it any less plausible. I continued before Wilson could interrupt. "Findlay could have killed Reilly before returning home. Reilly might have waited close by to switch clothes. They argued and Findlay left with the money. He was the only one who knew it existed."

Wilson tensed. His eyes glowed when they met mine. "That's the best idea I've heard all week. I'm going to run it past the M.E. Then, you're going to bring me the bracelet."

I made a quick escape before the detective arrested me for withholding evidence. Outside, I filled my lungs with fresh air. Three solid suspects for murder was better than one. Lorelei had opportunity and a strong enough motive for any jury. Haigh would never have let Reilly leave town without paying for Jensen's murder. Findlay was in this racket up to his hat brim. Too bad there was no way to prove who struck the fatal blows.

If the DA arrested Haigh or Findlay for murder, Lorelei was in the clear. My part in the case would be over.

Blank squares in my crossword puzzle stared at me.

I needed answers.

15

—·—

13 Across; 5 Letters
Clue: Containing nothing; a null set
Answer: Empty

It was late morning when I left the station. A touch early for lunch, but I didn't care. I couldn't think over my growling stomach. My phone buzzed. My worry faded when I saw a text from Kevin. "How about a sandwich?"

"Starving. A sandwich sounds wonderful. My usual."

Fifteen minutes later, I was at the top stair outside our apartment. I'd been picturing Kevin and I and our semi-romantic lunch alone. Once inside, I locked the door behind me. I was ready to be done with drama, cases, and crime.

In the kitchen, two pairs of eyes greeted me with smiles. Four if you counted the cats, but they appeared completely indifferent to my arrival.

I stopped in my tracks. "What is that child doing here?"

Marcus paused in pulling the sandwiches out of the sacks to give me a flat stare. "I live here, lady. I can play hooky when I want."

I crossed my arms over my chest. "Yes, to the first. A hard no to the second."

Kevin laughed and walked over to hug me. "Have you had a long day already?"

"I've spent hours dealing with Wilson and watching that tape. I have news." I leaned against him, returning his embrace. When I straightened, I leaned in for a kiss. "This is nice."

A moment later, my son cleared his throat. "Hello? Are we going to eat? Starving child here."

Hubby and I separated with a shared laugh.

Once seated, I eyed my gourmet veggie melt like it was my first love.

A jiggling door knob followed by a knock on the door interrupted my sandwich affair.

Marcus eyed me accusingly. "You locked the door?"

From the sound of his scathing tone, he couldn't have been more outraged if I'd brought a mountain lion home. Locking my front door wasn't a felony. I watched him jump up and cross the room to open the door. "I live here, fella. I can lock the door if I want."

Mrs. C wearing her pink fuzzy slippers sauntered in behind him.

"Where's Rabi?" I asked. "He'll miss the update."

"Here." The lean man walked through the open door with long strides. Being a deliveryman, he could set his own schedule for lunch.

I took a bite of my sandwich without waiting for the others to sit. I swallowed and gestured to the boy child with my glass of lemonade. "Why is he out of school?"

Kevin waved Marcus to silence when the boy opened his mouth. "I'll take this one. She's had a long day. Private contractors broke a gas main by the school. They shut off the gas, but school was dismissed to be safe. I gave myself the afternoon off."

Marcus eyed me. "What did the tape show? Is anyone getting arrested? You were supposed to text updates."

I gave a quick overview of my morning, including my and Wilson's theories based on the surprising Reilly, Findlay position swap.

My son slammed down his iced tea. "I did not see that coming. Are you sure?"

"Of that one thing, yes. It's too subtle for Findlay to fake." I swirled a handmade potato chip in the ketchup. "I'm not sure of anything else. If the M.E. says the time of death works, Findlay could be on the hotseat. Haigh, too. He might have been caught in the blast after killing Reilly."

Marcus's brow furrowed as I filled in the details. "That gets Lorelei off the hook. Is your puzzle finished?"

Faced with the question I'd been avoiding asking myself all afternoon, I took refuge in chewing on my potato chip. "Lorelei is still in the running. There's no proof who struck the fatal blows."

Mrs. C tapped his arm. "Best we wait till you can get it on the board, eh? I'll never remember the details otherwise, will I?"

"Me, too." Rabi agreed quickly as Marcus did a dance in his chair.

I winked at them both in gratitude for buying me time. My brain needed to digest the new clues and my body required fuel to run the whole process.

An hour later, after time out for eating, the new information graced the board along with new questions.

Marcus was still frowning. He looked as confused as I felt. "Why did he and Findlay switch places?"

Rabi looked over his steepled fingers. "Findlay had to plant the bomb."

We'd discussed many of the same theories Wilson and I had dredged up. I couldn't let the matter go. The answer had to be in front of me if only I put the questions in the correct order.

Mrs. C shook her head full of curls. The knitting needles clicked away. "What was the weapon? Why did Reilly return if he had the money and the bracelet? Your theory doesn't explain the loose threads, does it, luv?"

"No, it doesn't." My breath hissed through my gritted teeth. None of my theories contained all the answers. My brain whirled as the clues and answers circled each other in my mind. "Why did he return to Langsdale on Monday? He was already out of town. He came home for a reason."

"The bearer bonds?" Mrs. C pressed her lips together, emphasizing the wrinkles around her mouth. "The money he squirreled away to fund his life, eh? That would explain his return."

With my gaze on the board, I put my hand on Kevin's arm. "What do you think about Reilly's mindset? Why did he come to town?"

Kevin's expression grew distant as he looked into his past. "Getting away with the money before anyone knows you're gone is the hard part of the game. Reilly returned for the money."

Marcus put his knees on the chair and leaned over the table. "Reilly had the briefcase with him at the airport."

"No, he didn't. Honor among thieves is a myth." My hubby threw back his head and laughed. "Findlay kept the bracelet when Reilly left town or he kept the case. Neither man had both at any time."

"Of course." My puzzle was almost complete. The fresh outlook explained a great deal. "That's too much money to trust anyone with. Like the scorpion said to the frog as they were going down for the last time, 'You knew what I was when you picked me up.' No one involved in this was an innocent."

His blue eyes met mine. "They rarely are."

Marcus pointed at the list of suspects. "How did the bracelet get on the cat?"

A quick glance around the table showed only confusion, no answers to the question.

Rabi's dark eyes studied me. "Answers in a crossword puzzle interact with each other."

An electric jolt shot through me as his words lodged in my brain. The reminder that the solution, in puzzles as in murders, interacts with every other clue captured my attention as nothing else could have. "Everything was a moving target that night. Reilly and Findlay were probably switching clothes when Kevin and I were talking to Lorelei in the kitchen."

Mrs. C hadn't forgotten her knitting. The clicking alternately sped up and slowed as facts and ideas were presented.

Marcus sat. He stuck his chin between both fists. "How does all this rattle your theories?"

"I'm working them out." Motives and movement had confused me from the first hour in this case. "It comes down to people's nature. In the end, they can't change who they are. I think-"

My cell phone's loud ringing interrupted me. I swiped my thumb across the screen and answered. "Wilson, what's up?"

"The DA wants that bracelet *now*." He spaced each word evenly, clipping each one tightly.

I checked the time. "I still have most of an hour on our agreement."

"You're out of time." The detective's tone got harsher with each syllable. "Bring that bracelet in so we can examine it or I'll come and take possession of it."

"I'll be there." I wasn't about to surrender the only piece of evidence I had. Marcus and Kevin had found the bracelet fair and square on our rescue cat, who was staring at me across the table with her little gray paws on top of the table. I jabbed my finger at the feline offender.

Marcus pretended to be shocked and grabbed Rookie, cradling her in his arms. She batted at his face, again showing no claws, just a pair of over-toed paws.

My brain locked on a plan. "Can you get the Reilly daughters and Tiffany Sweet to the station? Also, the Findlays?"

"I'll get them here." Wilson's voice carried a thread of steel. "Are you planning a scene where you accuse the suspects like your hero, Hercule Poirot?"

"Why not?" I loved Agatha Christie books. Why not steal a scene from the queen of crime? Honestly, I was stewing on the clues and answers. The solution was in the puzzle, just beyond my reach. "And the gang's coming with me."

His yell cut off when I ended the call.

My bark of laughter relieved my tension for a heartbeat. Then I cast a sideways glance at Rabi. A blur was already hurtling toward my head. I grabbed the bracelet out of the air.

The metal back showed the engraved letters on the sections just as Marcus and I had connected them. A to A. B to B. C to C. All the way to J.

A flip to the jeweled side showed the electric connection in lines of orange, yellow, and red with small, matching jewels.

Mr. Pickles, not wanting to be left out, had jumped on Kevin's lap. He stood on his hind feet. His front paws kneaded Kevin's shoulder.

My hubby scratched the cat's ears. His eyes were as calm as a summer sky. A lifetime of high-stakes games had built that steel plank in his character.

A possibility hit me. I searched my memory for a detail that had been buried amid the weight of other facts. There was another possibility. I eyed Rabi, Mrs. C, and Marcus. "Grace under pressure."

The lean man nodded knowingly.

"Not everyone has the nerves to survive a fire fight or face down a mark." My body tensed for battle. Follow the clues. Complete the puzzle. As long as the answers meshed, down and across, I was good.

Marcus jumped up so suddenly Rookie twisted out of his arms and landed several feet away. "Let's go! I always wanted to have the big showdown."

Mrs. C frowned as she collected her knitting. "We've done that once or twice already, haven't we?"

I tossed the bracelet to Rabi as I stood. "Let's see who blinks first. I'm not so sure the contents of that briefcase hold the key to the murder."

16

— · —

62 Down; 12 Letters

Clue: A plan or scheme to outwit an opponent

Answer: Manipulation

Wilson swept his long arm around the meeting room. "The family and friends of the dear, departed Mr. Thaddeus Reilly. All gathered together."

Amy Reilly sat with her sister and brother-in-law, Bev and Jeremy Newcomb along one side of the long meeting table, facing me and Wilson.

Brooke and Paul Findlay had taken the head of the table to my right, next to each other. The woman was an elegant silver blonde. Her makeup, hair, and outfit were perfectly tailored. In nineteenth-century England, she'd have made a great duchess.

Tiffany sat by herself to the right of Jeremy and her nieces. A strain showed around the older woman's eyes, a testimony to her illness.

I don't know what strings Wilson had to pull to allow this confrontation. However, the mayor and the DA were pushing for a solution. They'd give the detective a lot of leeway.

Wilson looked even more like a scarecrow when he folded his tall, lanky frame against the door. He jerked his head to the table where the briefcase sat. "The floor is yours, Belden."

Rabi had returned the bracelet to me. I clutched it in my hand. I spun to face the Findlays showing them the jeweled image. "This is what you've been looking for isn't it, Brooke?"

Paul Findlay, with his large, heavy frame, looked like a blacksmith next to her.

Brooke's stiff smile didn't reach her eyes. "I was looking for my husband's property. Thaddeus gave him that bracelet."

I pointed at her husband. "This is the piece you needed? You lost it Monday morning at the Reilly house."

"I don't know what you're talking about." The strain of holding onto his patience showed in his tight tone. "Thaddeus and I had an agreement."

"No doubt." I chortled at his words. "Cue the frog."

A round of frowns greeted me. Everyone except the members of the Belden-Tanner Agency.

"I'll get to that later." I pointed to the wall behind me and Wilson. A red drape had been opened to reveal a thick plexiglass window. A workroom could be seen beyond the glass. The briefcase was encased in another plexiglass cell; eight-foot-by-eight-foot.

Two members of the bomb squad stood at the corner of the cell. Both were dressed in the bulky protection outfits of their unit. Evidently, a sign of trust in my judgment. More likely they were the epitome of the always-be-prepared crowd.

"Marcus and I rearranged the bracelet." I held up the evidence in my hands. "We discovered that when the sections are in the proper order it gives off an electric charge."

Wilson stared through the window. "What do you think?"

One of the bomb squad guys eyed Wilson. "The charges will only blow if you try to force the lock."

Wilson gave him a nod. "Try it."

Silence reigned as I passed the bracelet to a waiting officer. The man on the bomb squad entered the small cell and used a mechanical arm to hold the metallic key next to the lock on the case. In the breathless silence, the satisfying click caused several gasps around the table.

The bomb squad guy moved closer, beckoning his teammate forward. "We'll disarm the traps."

"Good idea." Wilson gave me a look of appreciation. "Good job, Tracy. Now, what's with this frog business?"

I gave a brief overview of the old story. "Halfway across the river the scorpion stings the frog, knowing they'll both die. When the frog asks why, the scorpion says he had to be true to his nature. Reilly was brilliant and he wanted the world to know it. No one was as important as him and his success. Am I close, Tiffany?"

His sister eyed me with a steady, resigned expression. "He always had to win. People were like pieces on a game board. There to serve his climb to the top."

"Ready." The bomb squad man entered the meeting room and handed the case to Wilson.

Brooke and Paul Findlay exchanged sharp, hungry looks. They looked like springs ready to jump to out of their skins.

Lorelei was quicker. Sitting on my side of the table, she was already on her feet. Her gaze was glued to the briefcase. Her hands were pressed against her ribcage, directly under her heart. "How much are we talking about?"

Straight to the bottom line. A wave of admiration came over me. On this point, Lorelei was a woman after my own heart. With my neutral mask in place, I met Kevin's amused gaze.

I fought back a grin. "How much money?"

After a moment of searching glances, Paul Findlay found himself the center of attention. Findlay tightened his jaw. An obstinate look burned in his eyes.

"Don't mess with me." Wilson's knuckles hit the table with a rapport that sounded like a bullet. "Answer the question."

They glowered at each other but I had no doubt who would cave.

In a matter of seconds, the accountant's militancy wilted before the scarecrow's withering stare.

Findlay's gaze fell. He waved at the case with a dispirited air. "The hidden accounts plus the bearer bonds total eleven million dollars."

That sucked the air right out of the room.

My whole body jerked in surprise. Stunned didn't begin to explain how I felt. "Reilly accumulated that much money in five years?"

The octave I reached sounded suspiciously close to Lorelei at her most hysterical. I started to wonder about my life choices, then my gaze landed on my little family standing by the door.

Pale green eyes. Two pairs of black eyes, one young, one older. And the one bright blue gaze I'd known for over a decade. Each one understood my reaction. I glanced at the case and smiled. It was nice to dream, but I wouldn't change anything.

Findlay's mouth settled into a frown. He stared at me with a furious look.

Why do people get angry at *me*? All I do is solve puzzles.

Beverly leapt to her feet. "Where did he get that money? Not from my company."

Possessive, isn't she? Good thing Daddy wasn't still around.

"Don't worry." Findlay leaned back in his chair. "He's accumulated the funds since college. Padding bids. Siphoning off up-charges. Then he got into high-risk stock trades. Off the table deals. Everything he touched turned to gold."

Jealousy underlay each word.

Wilson crossed his arms over his chest.

The accountant touched the case with his fingers. "Thaddeus tucked money away for twenty years. With compound interest, it built up."

"That makes me feel better."

Everyone around the table frowned at me.

"Glad to hear it." Wilson scoffed. "This is all about you."

"Hello?" Lorelei waved her arms. "Who does this case and the contents legally belong to?"

Wilson put on his professional mask. "That will be up to the lawyers who settle the estate. Open it."

He pointed to Findlay, who was closest.

The entire room seemed to hold its breath.

Findlay grabbed the lid and threw the case open. With a rustle of paper, he pulled out an over-sized brown envelope, then shoved the case away.

Jeremy tensed and put his arm in front of Beverly when the briefcase slid in their direction.

I gave the man five stars for his protective gesture. As the case stopped at the edge of the table, he knocked it away.

The accountant tore open the envelope. Longing. Lust. Years of work... and now, he'd never touch his share of the money. He threw the documents the length of the table. A stream of paper colored the varnished wood. "So close."

Paul Findlay's frown darkened his expression.

Lorelei tapped her lacquered nails on the table as she wrapped a curl around her finger. "Do be careful with those."

Beverly reared to her feet. "You only get what you were promised in my father's will. Not one penny more."

"He was my husband." Lorelei choked up on the last word. Her chin quivered. She was good. Then the not-so-grieving widow put out a pouty lip followed by her sweetest smile. "We'll talk later."

That would be an interesting interaction.

"Now, it's my turn." I wiggled my fingers. Every gaze shifted to me like the audience at a tennis match. "No one has asked why Reilly was squirreling this money away. Although his accountant knows."

Findlay's brow furrowed in perfect confusion.

I met his puzzled gaze. He didn't flinch, not one blink. "He helped his client hide a crime."

Findlay's outrage was immediate and flawless. "I know nothing of the kind. His money was obtained legally. Profits from his own company. Extra contracts."

"He hid the money from me." Anger hardened Lorelei's hair-raising voice as she over-rode the man's self-defense. "Those funds wouldn't have been counted in a divorce."

"Thaddeus never discussed his reasons and I never asked." Findlay reared to his feet. "He was a client. He wanted to move money around. It's his business."

I rested my hands on the back of an empty chair. "You didn't know why he was stashing money?"

"What *was* his plan?" Beverly's screech had everyone jerking in surprise as she leapt to her feet.

Everyone jumped, even the bomb guy.

"Tell me." She inched toward her father's old friend. "What were the two of you up to?"

Findlay stared at her with wide eyes. Faced with another Reilly demanding an answer, he caved, again. "Thaddeus had several identities set up."

"He was going to skip out on me?" Lorelei, also on her feet, filled her lungs. With her hands fisted, she opened her mouth.

"Sit down. Everyone." Wilson pointed to Lorelei's chair. He swept the room with a commanding expression. Once the others took their seats, he focused on Paul Findlay. "You have no alibi for Reilly's murder."

The man's face went slack. "What are you saying?"

Wilson gestured to me without turning around.

I pointed at the television where the detective had previously played the tape of the convenience store. "Reilly is the one on the film from the convenience store. I can prove it. Which means you were at the house. Lorelei smacked you with the bat. I'm betting you have a bump on your head."

Wilson withdrew a folded blue paper from his jacket "I have a court order for you to be examined by a doctor."

"Have his head examined." The trill of Mrs. C's giggle was joined by the muffled laugh of a boy.

I bit my cheek to swallow the laughter bubbling up in my throat.

Wilson appeared unfazed by the theatrics. "The M.E. is waiting down the hall. You want to do this the hard way?"

Findlay held up under the detective's scrutiny for a long moment. When Wilson pointed to the door, the other man slumped. "Lorelei hit me. I planted the bomb. I had the home owner's permission. That can't be a crime."

Did he actually believe that or was he planning his defense for insanity?

Mrs. C's giggle cut across the dramatic diatribe. "The dead man has an alibi. That's rich, eh?"

I had to bite my lip and cover my mouth to hide my smile. The old woman was going to be the death of me. She was totally undermining my control.

Findlay bared his teeth in her direction. At least she was undermining his control, too. "The plan was to split the stash. He'd disappear and I'd live off of my half. No one would know."

The detective stopped in his tracks. He studied Findlay with a narrowed gaze. "But eleven million is better than five, by killing him you get it all."

The other man leaned forward. His hands splayed before him on the table. "Thaddeus had the briefcase. I had the bracelet that unlocked it. After Lorelei hit me, I wasn't sure I'd recover. One of the cats was licking my face. Without thinking it through, I put the bracelet around the cat's neck. I couldn't risk the police or the hospital taking it off me."

An answer for my puzzle. "That explains the eleven-million-dollar cat collar."

Findlay cast an accusing look at Lorelei. "She was gone so long, my head cleared. The cat was nowhere to be found. I stumbled off to meet Thaddeus."

"The best laid plans…" I let the words trail away. "All his scheming and neither of you could touch the money."

"When I told him what happened, he was furious." The accountant gave a harsh laugh. "He was determined to salvage something. He stalked off toward the house. I reminded him about the bomb and the timer. I was done. I got in my car and drove home."

Amy raked both hands through her dark hair. "Why would our father blow up his house?"

"To sow confusion so he could disappear." Beyond all the hysteria, none of them had a clue about Reilly's true motive. "Brandon Haigh threatened and fought with Reilly for years. Their quarrel escalated in the past few months. Your father was on a short timer to escape before his crimes were uncovered."

Tiffany Sweet's mouth fell open. Her nieces shared her look of astonishment. The dead man's sister gripped her cane till her knuckles turned white. "What are you talking about?"

"Embezzlement. Murder." I counted the crimes on my fingers as I spoke. "The first one doesn't matter, statute of limitations and all, but murder? That's gonna bite you, Mr. Findlay."

"Another murder?" Findlay jerked as if I'd tased him. His eyes grew wide. "I know nothing of any crimes."

I kept my smile inward behind a know-it-all expression.

"It comes down to human nature." The frog and the scorpion had put me on the right track. "Reilly had talent but he took a shortcut on the ladder of success."

In short sentences, I painted the picture of Lester Jensen's embezzlement, Reilly's copycat crime, and my version of their fatal confrontation. I included Jensen's alleged resting place in the foundation of the Drake. As a final touch, I laid out how Haigh pegged Reilly as a murderer.

Shocked expressions greeted my revelation.

"Haigh was by the house that night." The skin around Findlay's eyes tightened at my barb. "He was injured in the blast."

Brooke stared at her husband. Shock and confusion chased each other across her face.

Wilson continued. "That's how Reilly ended up in the open area behind his house. But you were with him. You're a big man. When he lost his temper, you could have taken him down."

The accused man stiffened. "He was alive when I drove away. After that I never left my house."

The detective was undeterred. He flung out his arm. "You learned the electrician's and demolition skills in your construction work. You could have re-wired your security system to leave a window or door off the grid."

Findlay appeared surprisingly calm. The smile on his face was one usually reserved for a beautiful sunset. "When he stalked away and I drove off, it was like a weight had lifted off my shoulders. The money had blinded me to everything else. It wasn't worth one more step. I don't regret leaving without the bonds."

The Sierra Madre movie would have been vastly different if anyone had learned that lesson.

Brooke grabbed her husband's arm. She studied his face with a glacial expression. "At one point, I contemplated how I could kill him. Greed consumes you."

Her shoulders melted until she collapsed against him.

Wilson rapped his knuckles on the table. "There's the issue of planting a bomb, destroying property, endangering lives, not to mention murder."

"I did the rest of it." Findlay tore his gaze away from his wife. "But I never touched him."

The detective looked over his shoulder at me. "I believe him."

I nodded in turn. It was disappointing, but I couldn't lie. "So do I."

"How can you say that?" Jeremy was on his feet, ignoring Beverly's restraining hand. "You force us to come here. You put us through this wringer of emotions and you get it wrong?"

"I never accused Paul Findlay of murder." I wanted that on record. I pointed to Wilson. "Police are allowed to lie to suspects. They do it all the time."

Wilson nodded without a sign of regret. "I could spin a story where each of you might be the killer."

Jeremy stepped toward me almost sputtering. "You staged all of this and you don't know which of us is the killer."

"Yes, I do." I pointed to the other side of the table. "Tiffany, the grieving sister, murdered her brother."

The woman in question drew back as if I'd struck her. "Why would I kill Thaddeus?"

"Because he murdered your husband, Sam." I hadn't liked Reilly when he was alive. Nothing I'd learned since his death had improved my opinion of him. But judging isn't my job. Lorelei hired me to find her husband's murderer. "I'm guessing he let something slip about the supposed accident that killed his wife and your husband."

I ignored the second round of shocked expressions to focus on the woman I'd just accused of murder. "He wasn't headed *to* your house. You and he were walking away *from* your house when he was killed."

Tiffany met my gaze head on. The weariness that had seemed to envelope her lifted. Her mouth tilted up in a smile. "For once in her life, Lorelei chose wisely."

"Thanks." My client's bubbly voice spoke quickly then cut off. "Hey, wait a minute."

I ignored the woman to keep my gaze on her sister-in-law. "What did Reilly say?"

"I knew my brother was cold hearted." Tiffany cast an apologetic look at Reilly's family and friends. "But I had no idea he killed anyone. Let alone that he made a habit of it."

Both of her nieces edged closer to their aunt.

Their aunt faced them. "I'd had a few drinks before I went to bed. He woke me out of a sound sleep babbling about needing money. He was almost hysterical. I got dressed and went into the living room."

Tiffany eyed her nieces. "He'd worked himself into a frenzy. He was screaming how the universe had always provided what he needed at the perfect time. A wet road, a patsy for missing money-"

She snapped her fingers and pointed at me.

"The embezzlement." I interjected. "Lester was his scapegoat."

"I just got it." Tiffany sighed. "The other reference I understood right away. Icy roads."

Beverly paled. "Icy... what?"

Amy gasped as her hands covered her mouth.

Tiffany's lips thinned. "He didn't even catch his slip-up. As he turned away he had a satisfied look on his face. I couldn't breathe. The car crash that killed Carol and Sam... the man I loved more than my life, was blamed on icy conditions. It was like a bomb exploded in my brain. There was no accident. He was driving, and he murdered them."

When the silence stretched out, I interjected what I knew. "The headlines about the car crash highlighted the death of his wife. My agency members read several articles to the very last paragraph to learn that Samuel Sweet, Reilly's brother-in-law also died."

Tiffany pressed a hand to her heart. "We lived in the hills around Lake Tahoe at the time. The weather report had called for a freeze all week. It rained in the afternoon but Thaddeus insisted on coming with Carol to our house for supper, driving up that winding road. He was flying out of town the next day. He'd be gone for three weeks."

The woman blinked rapidly. She paused as she swallowed hard. "As Thaddeus and Carol were leaving, Sam got word his truck was repaired. He insisted Thaddeus drop him off. The garage was on their way."

The woman fell silent as if reliving that night was too much to handle.

"The car struck the tree on the passenger side. Reilly was injured. The other two were killed on impact." I'd had long enough to work out the pieces on the way over and during Findlay's confession. "Reilly was on the short list to head a prestigious, but conservative non-profit corporation. The death of his wife would put him in the national limelight. He'd garner sympathy. That would never happen if Carol filed for divorce and proved him guilty of infidelity."

"Which she would have," Lorelei interjected. "He was a hound, everyone knew it."

My client's mention of the earlier affairs had added the motive to Reilly's second and third murders. My gaze remained on Reilly's sister. "The ice on the road would be gone by the time Reilly returned from his trip. For him, the moment was too perfect to pass up, even if another innocent had to die. A later accident on a dry road might put Reilly under suspicion. He made sure to hit the tree on the passenger side. His speed was estimated at over sixty miles an hour."

"I was in a daze." Tiffany reached her hands out to her nieces. "I didn't know what to do. He was babbling about how Paul had destroyed his master plan."

The Findlays clasped hands as they stared at the woman.

A strangled chuckle escaped Tiffany's set jaw. "Thaddeus kept whining about fate turning against him. He demanded I give him the money I had in my safe. Then he ordered me to liquidate the rest of my holdings on Monday and send him the entire amount until he figured something out."

"That's when you decided." Wilson prompted her.

Tiffany nodded. "I told him I left my car in the lot by the trail and Amy dropped me off. She did sometimes. He didn't even stop to think. He had a plane to catch."

Wilson's eyes narrowed. "No tickets under his *real* name."

"One of his other identities." I added the tidbit since Tiffany seemed lost in memories of murder and the loss of her love. "Your nieces told me your health is failing. When I spoke to you the next morning, you used the wall and a table for support, but the stand by the door had no canes in it."

Both of the younger women shot me accusing looks.

That didn't stop me. "When Grandad's gout kicked in, my aunts and uncles bought him a cane with a metal carving on top."

Which would be perfect for the still missing murder weapon.

Tiffany, unlike her scowling nieces, gave me a wink. "As we left, I picked up my walking stick topped with a heavy knob of silver."

The last few answers in my puzzle fell into place. "He trusted you. He walked into a dip in the grassy area. One good swing would have put him on his knees."

"He was never sorry for the people he hurt as long as he came out looking good." Tiffany's gaze grew distant. Tears coursed down her cheeks. "I kept hitting him and hitting him."

I found my hands clasping the back of the chair in a white-knuckled grip. I'd rarely felt sympathy for a killer before. However, I can't say I would have acted differently. Considering her health, I also doubted Tiffany would spend any time in jail. With enough delays, she might not live to see a trial.

As Wilson walked toward Tiffany Sweet, Amy rushed around the table to embrace her aunt. Beverly followed at a more sedate pace, holding Jeremy's hand. A calculating expression stiffened her features.

I felt like a dishrag. I turned to my family and friends with a handy exit at their back.

Kevin stepped up and put an arm around my shoulders.

"Can I leave now?" Lorelei's voice sounded behind me.

I knew she was talking to me. All I could do was fight for the strength not to strangle the woman.

"Tracy." Lorelei spoke in an imperious tone. "Do I get those bonds?"

Kevin looked over my head with a steady look. "This case is over. Lose her number."

A gasp sounded behind me.

My hero. I rewarded my hubby with a smile.

Rabi held the door open.

Mrs. C and Marcus didn't even try to hide their grins.

I put my arm around Kevin's waist and we walked forward. "Let's go home."

17

— • —

47 Down; 7 Letters
Clue: For all time
Answer: Forever

Later that day, supper had come and gone but talk of murder remained. The Belden Agency was arrayed comfortably around the sectional.

I was frankly too tired to move. Talk had circled of starting a movie but no one had enough initiative to make a decision. Tomorrow was a school day. It was also adoption day. Kevin had mentioned keeping Marcus home. I was all for it. Either way, it was getting late.

When I said as much, Marcus rolled over on the couch. "You're only saying that because you're almost asleep."

Rabi smiled. "Past my bedtime."

My son's laughter was interrupted by a knock on the door. He sat up, bright-eyed and instantly alert. "Who's that?"

Kevin gathered himself to stand.

I groaned since I was laying against him.

Rabi waved him back. "I'll get it."

"Check who it is." Marcus stabbed a finger as he whispered the warning.

The lean man responded with a wink and looked through the peephole.

"It's Wilson." The detective's raised voice sounded through the door. "I come bearing gifts."

"Oh good. Update on the arrest, eh?" Mrs. C drew herself straighter as well, blinking the sleep out of her eyes. "Do let the man in."

A second later, the man crossed the threshold. He held out a blue and gold package. "A Silver Streak Creamery Ice Cream Cake."

"Yeah!" Before the word died, Marcus had jumped to his feet, swooped the package out of Wilson's hands, and was halfway to the kitchen.

Mrs. C pushed herself to her feet. "I'd best oversee this whole affair."

The detective looked at his suddenly empty hands then exchanged a nod of greeting with Rabi. With the door shut behind him, Wilson advanced into the room. His narrowed gaze studied Rookie, stretched out on the sectional. The cat stared back. Mr. Pickles flicked a glance at the man from his post on the scratching tree then dismissed him.

Wilson raised a brow. "The animal shelter, I hear."

"Yeah." Kevin imbued the single word with a wealth of casual sincerity. He helped me to my feet then he looked straight at lanky, sandy haired detective. "The one on the south side has a lot of cats if you're interested."

The detective stared at my hubby. Then, he shook himself and faced me. "Why do I believe him when I know you never went to that shelter?"

"It's his superpower." I waved both men toward the kitchen and the ice-cream cake. "If it's any comfort, I would have bought his version, too."

Kevin smiled over his shoulder. "Every good line is based on the truth. To make the sell, you have to *believe*."

"Come on, people." Marcus's command was accompanied by several resounding slaps on the table top. "We need the update from police headquarters."

I dismissed Wilson's hesitant expression with a wave. "If you didn't want to spill your guts, you shouldn't have come."

The detective shrugged. "I owe you for this collar."

Mrs. C slid a piece of ice-cream cake onto a plate. "Aye, there's a lot of truth in that bit."

Wilson took the comment and his ice-cream treat with a smile. He spooned off a bite and moaned in delight. "I love these cakes."

My son pointed his spoon at the man. "Spill. I may not have much time left before being forced to go to bed. What happened after we left?"

"Tough crowd." The detective took a seat. "Lorelei gave her statement. She's been released. Bev promised to double the amount in the will if she went quietly. One word and Bev swore to fight her. Lorelei agreed to sign the papers in the morning. Tiffany Sweet was arrested, charged with murder, and released on her own recognizance."

I listened as I chewed on a bite of chocolate cookie crust, fudge swirl ice cream, mocha ganache, and crushed toffee. "Has Beverly brought in a defense lawyer yet?"

"Why am I here?" Wilson spoke around a mouthful of ice cream before swallowing. "You were out of the room before she said a word."

Kevin scoffed. "Not before Amy bolted around the table to hug her aunt. Any of that man's family and friends might have killed him. Tiffany got there first. They figure they owe her."

"I had Findlay pegged, maybe with his wife's help," Wilson admitted. "I could have made it stick."

The statement was not an idle boast. "The case against Findlay had a lot going for it. A jury might have convicted any of them, including Lorelei."

"Especially her." Mrs. C look up from putting extra chocolate sauce on her cake. "What put you onto the sister, then?"

"The manner of death." Several details from the coroner's report had stuck with me. "Findlay had the size and strength to take Reilly down, but the placement of the blows didn't work for me."

Wilson grimaced. "It worked to kill him."

I licked my spoon clean then shook it at the man. "You never had to sneak up on bigger, older brothers and attack them with a plastic pool noodle."

Everyone in the room looked at me like I was crazy.

Who knew? "Anyway, raising both arms above your head is too obvious. It's better to hold it by your leg and smack them from below. Or wait on the stairs and get above them."

Marcus smacked his forehead. "A sneak attack, everyone knows that."

"Of course, luv." Mrs. C saluted me with a forkful of ice cream. "Frontal assault is much more obvious, isn't it?"

I forgot who I was talking to. No more game analogies. Next time I'll go with crime or war. "When we were headed to the police station earlier, Kevin and Rabi walking side-by-side reminded me of Reilly and Findlay. Both sets of men are roughly the same height. When Findlay was talking, I realized what was bothering me. If Rabi decided to kill Kevin-"

"Whoa there, cowgirl." Kevin held up a hand. "Rabi has enough on his scorecard. I want to be the killer."

I opened my mouth to comment on the mental age of the combatants, then thought better of it. "Fine, in this analogy you can kill Rabi."

The victim in question eyed Kevin. "You can try."

As everyone laughed, I motioned the former Special Ops vet to his feet and stood slightly behind him. "Kevin would bring the weapon in from the side and behind, not on top of his skull. That didn't mesh with the M.E.'s report."

Wilson's gaze narrowed. "The damage to Reilly's skull was all on top and on one side."

I pointed my spoon at him. "The only way for anyone to strike the top of his skull was for him to be in a ditch. Reilly wouldn't have turned his back on another man, either Findlay or Haigh. It *had* to be a woman."

Kevin tapped his index finger on the table. "Why not the daughters or Brooke Findlay?"

"Multiple blows." That's what had killed the dead man. "That's a lot of bottled-up rage. Tiffany said she knew what her brother was like, but they all knew."

Wilson's expression was pensive. "This attack was explosive."

"Findlay wanted the money. He'd have been happy with over five million dollars. Haigh wanted to destroy Reilly's reputation by revealing him as a heartless killer." I twirled my spoon. "That's when I remembered the death of Tiffany's husband. For Reilly, his wife's death was convenient. Tiffany raised the girls. He got the seat on the board. He was free."

Wilson leaned forward. "Reilly was driving the car. He was badly injured. No one ever considered he caused the accident."

"It hit the tree on the passenger side. As the driver, he was in total control of the speed and the angle of the impact."

"Dadgummit." Marcus fisted his hands. "We all read about that accident and the money. I guess that's why you get the big bucks."

"And I earned it." I was happy to put the case behind me. "I had to spend a week following Reilly. I saw firsthand how self-centered he was."

"He killed Lester Jensen to hide his own embezzlement. Then, he murdered his wife and brother-in-law." Marcus frowned. "That's sick."

The police detective took his last bite of ice-cream cake. "As an officer, I don't judge the guilty party. However, Beverly has hired the best defense lawyer in the west. They're going for a diminished capacity defense. With Tiffany's cancer spreading, she won't see trial."

"One good thing came from this case." Marcus paused to feed Mr. Pickles and Rookie a piece of the chocolate cookie crust.

Everyone waited in anticipation of his pronouncement.

"We have two cats who are going to live with us forever."

"Forever, you say?" I tried to keep a fierce tone while I stared at my boy child. A bite of ice cream melted on my spoon. "When did I agree to forever?"

My son's lips quivered. He raised a brow while struggling to look serious. "Forever was part of the contract when you chased me down years ago."

Kevin snorted as he fought to contain his laughter. "You two were made for each other."

Marcus and I turned on him as one, but the boy was faster with the comeback. "You're part of this, mister."

"And so are you and you." I flung my arms out and pointed to Mrs. C and Rabi in turn. "We're all in this... together. Forever."

Rabi smiled. "Deal."

"Absolutely, luv." Mrs. C nodded serenely. "None of us are going anywhere else, are we?"

Marcus's face lit up. His expression held a touch of smugness about it.

18

— • —

9 Down; 6 Letters
Clue: A set of people related by blood or affection
Answer: Family

I have to say, the Astoria Golden Ballroom lived up to the hype. Hanging on Kevin's arm, I stared at the gold stars painted on the dark blue ceiling like I was six years old.

Swirling golden borders surrounded paintings of galaxies and comets blazing through the night sky. Other murals displayed mountain ranges, colorful sunsets of amber and orange, and the soft dunes of the desert. The French doors along the far wall were open to a view of the real landscape made the setting come alive.

Marcus nudged me without looking away from the ceiling. "When the lights go down, all of the stars start to glow. That should be way cool."

I hugged Kevin's arm. "I can't believe it. The adoption day finally happened. Marcus is ours, for good."

"Or bad." The boy child interjected with a laugh.

Kevin turned a smiling face to me. "Till death do us part. We're family now. All of us."

Marcus smiled over his shoulder, stopping as Rabi and Mrs. C caught up to us.

No one could stop smiling. We'd come directly from the court house where the judge had read the official adoption decree. Then, at Marcus's insistence, she'd called up Rabi and Mrs. C and entered into the official record that they were also members of the family and as such were responsible for Marcus Belden-Tanner.

After another group hug, I glanced around the small ballroom. Suitable for one hundred fifty guests; half that if a dance floor was needed.

Blue and silver decorations met the eye everywhere from the centerpieces on the tables to the large poles adorned with balloons and streamers.

Marcus's eyes grew big as took it all in. "I'm glad the bride didn't pick pink."

I looked at the buffet table set against one wall. "I hope they picked good food."

Mom and Pop joined us. They'd surprised Marcus by flying in this morning and had been with us at the courthouse. They planned to stay for the weekend.

"Hey, Partner." Pop held up a big, callused hand.

Marcus popped forward with a resounding high five. "Hey, Grandad. It's official now."

Mom pulled the boy in for a hug. "When you all come down in June, we can celebrate the wedding and your adoption."

The boy child threw his arms up in the air. "More parties! More presents!"

A couple of his classmates and their families arrived. Followed by two of his teachers. The entire class had been invited.

"Hey!" Crawford's bellow echoed throughout the ballroom. His wide frame was silhouetted in the doorway. He had a wide face and a forehead lined with furrows. His sandy blond hair was combed straight back. "Is this where the Belden-Tanner party is? I've waited a long time for this day."

I waved and smiled in greeting. "The others are coming?"

Roxie, Crawford's admin, ran past him like a red-headed tornado. With her high-heels clattering against the floor, she caught Marcus in a tight embrace, squealing as she spun him around. "I'm so happy this day is finally here."

Marcus pulled back, his straight black hair in sharp contrast to her red curls. "Did you tell everyone?"

The young woman's grin grew wider. "You bet I did. This has been years in the making. No one should show up empty handed."

As a familiar line of our friends filed in the doorway, I saw boxes and gift bags in each of their hands. Rickson, a six-foot-eight-inch operative I've worked with on a few cases, shook a two-foot square box over his head while yelling at Marcus.

Jimbo, Kevin's friend, with his boyfriend Nathan were right behind him. Wilson, along with several detectives and uniform officers also filed in. Mrs. C greeted her book club members with a piercing call and rushed forward. Our neighbors mixed with the police department's finest. Presents filled all of their hands.

I fisted my hands on my hips. "Marcus, you can't ask people for presents."

The boy copied my stance and thrust his shoulders forward. A taunting smile spread across his face. "I didn't. Roxie did."

I caught my breath and fought a failing battle to hide my laughter.

"How often does a guy get adopted?" Marcus cast a conspiratorial look at me and Kevin. "There'll be presents for you, too."

"Really?" I tried to act casual but my smile broke out. "Perhaps we shouldn't make rules too quickly."

Who would have guessed that having a street thief steal my wallet would turn out to be one of the best days of my life? I would never have guessed that the twists and turns of life would bring me to this day.

With a hysterectomy behind me, I'd given up on being a mother, then fate, karma, or the universe put Marcus in my path. Over the past few years, he turned a group of loners into a family.

"This day has definitely been a long-awaited celebration." Kevin put a hand on our son's shoulder. "It took a lot of adventures to make us a family. And we have a lot of adventures ahead of us."

I put my arm around Mrs. C as Marcus knocked knuckles with Rabi. "The Belden Tanner Agency. Now, we're family. All of us."

LETTER TO READERS

Dear Readers,

I'm so happy to welcome new readers and wish a happy return to those who are familiar with Tracy and her adopted family! I'm also excited at the thought of anyone who gets this far and reads this letter.

How do you like the additions to the family: Rookie and Mr. Pickles? I didn't intend to add cats to the mix, but when they sauntered onto the page what could I do but add them to the family? The names of the cats, their description, and their toe-counts are based on two cats belonging to my granddaughters.

When I started the first book, I wanted to tell the story of Trixie Belden and her friends from the YA series as adults still solving mysteries. However, as I wrote the story, it turned out Tracy and her friends had their own story to tell.

I kept the Belden name as an homage to the series that started my love of mysteries. The wonderful response to the Belden name took me by surprise. However, it's been great fun to connect with other fans of the Trixie Belden mystery series, plus I've found fans of my own stories!

I hope you enjoy your time in Langsdale, Nevada. If you liked the book and have the time, please leave a review at Amazon, Goodreads, Bookbub, or anywhere you can think of; friends, family. Really, anywhere.

To learn how Tracy and Kevin met go to my website: www.louisefo
ster.com   and sign up for my newsletter. You'll get a FREE download
of their first adventure together: <u>One Across is Murder</u>

Thank you for giving me your support by buying this book and your
time by reading it. I don't take either for granted.

I hope you enjoyed this book and the others in the series.

Louise Foster

MEET THE AUTHOR

I didn't pursue a writing career until I was well out of college. However, a lifelong love of reading and solving puzzles proved to be good training. While I enjoy reading many different genres, from thrillers to fantasy to science fiction, mysteries have always intrigued me.

Working on jigsaw puzzles and crossword puzzles with my family has also been a constant part of my life. A habit that carries through to today.

In the Crossword Puzzle Mystery Series, my love of writing and solving puzzles came together. I hope you love the quirky characters and their high-spirited adventures as much as I enjoy writing them.

To learn more about the Crossword Puzzle Cozy Mystery series, visit my website and sign up for my newsletter. You can also solve a crossword puzzle related to each of the books as they're released on my website.

To read the other books in the Crossword Puzzle Cozy Mystery series visit the Amazon series page: https://www.amazon.com/gp/product/B098R27WX6?ref

My author page on Facebook is: Louise Foster Author | Facebook

I'd love to hear from you: Louise.louisefoster@gmail.com

ACKNOWLEDGMENTS

So many people helped bring my story to a published book. Thanks to:

My editor, Mary-Theresa Hussey, her wonderful input.

Lee Hyat, who created my beautiful book covers.

My writing group, Romance Authors of the Heartland.

ALSO BY LOUISE FOSTER

One Across is Death (Short Story Prequel) – *Tracy and Kevin meet for the first time when she finds him standing over her dead co-worker with the murder weapon at his feet. Tracy isn't sure the handsome stranger is guilty, but how can she solve this puzzle?*

A Clue to Murder (Novella Prequel) – Two years after Tracy and Kevin first meet, his landlords ask her to find their missing nephews. When her investigation leads to a dead body, she fears the worst for the missing teens. but she must find the boys and finish her puzzle. (Both prequels are available on my website when you sign up for my newsletter: www.louise foster.com)

An Ex in the Puzzle

Two Down in Tahoe

Adventures in Vegas

A Question of Murder

Five Clues to a Killer

Seven Furlongs to a Felony

Eight Letters in Betrayal

Glue Guns for Christmas (Novella)

www.ingramcontent.com/pod-product-compliance
Lightning Source LLC
Chambersburg PA
CBHW020610180626
46810CB00007B/2711